THE SPIRIT FLYER SERIES

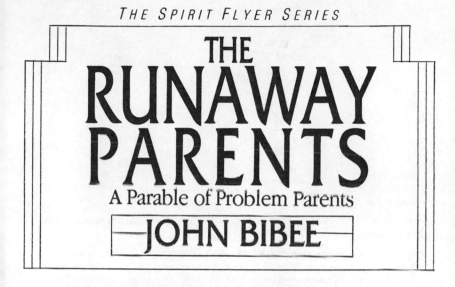

THE RUNAWAY PARENTS

A Parable of Problem Parents

JOHN BIBEE

Illustrated by Paul Turnbaugh

INTERVARSITY PRESS
DOWNERS GROVE, ILLINOIS 60515

InterVarsity Press is the book-publishing division of InterVarsity Christian Fellowship, a student movement active on campus at hundreds of universities, colleges and schools of nursing in the United States of America, and a member movement of the International Fellowship of Evangelical Students. For information about local and regional activities, write Public Relations Dept., InterVarsity Christian Fellowship, 6400 Schroeder Rd., P.O. Box 7895, Madison, WI 53707-7895.

Cover illustration: Paul Turnbaugh

ISBN 0-8308-1205-9

Printed in the United States of America

Library of Congress Cataloging-in-Publication Data
Bibee, John.
    The runaway parents: a parable of problem parents/John Bibee; illustrated by Paul Turnbaugh.
    p.   cm.—(The Spirit Flyer series; 6)
    Summary: The Kramar family is split apart when the parents decide to stop following the way of the Spirit Flyer Bicycles and join forces with the powerful and sinister Goliath Industries.
    ISBN 0-8308-1205-9
    [1. Fantasy.]   I. Turnbaugh, Paul, ill.   II. Title.   III. Series:
Bibee, John.   Spirit Flyer series; 6.
PZ7.B471464Ru   1991
   [Fic.]—dc20

                                             91-22762
                                             CIP
                                             AC

15	14	13	12	11	10	9	8	7	6	5	4	3	2	1
03	02	01	00	99	98	97	96	95	94	93	92	91		

For Martha and Faye

TWO LESTERS
COME
TO STAY
· · · · · · · · ·

1

Some people live in a place far away from their true home. Like exiles, they wander, searching for something that will satisfy their deep wishes and secret dreams. They try many roads, but until they pass through the roads in the Deeper World, they will never find their way home, and they will never eat at the table of their family and friends . . .

A new year of ORDER came to Centerville. Many people were saying it was a new age of peace and safety, but John Kramar didn't feel peaceful or safe or happy. He climbed out of a tiny bed and bumped his head on the ceiling.

"Rats!" John muttered angrily. Half asleep, he had forgotten he was staying in a tiny room in the attic. It was hardly a room at all, as much as it was just a storage space, John thought with disgust. There was a bed that was too soft and very creaky, and an ancient dresser with a tall cracked mirror. An old brass lamp stand with a single bulb stood by the lonely little bed. The rest of the space was filled with cardboard boxes, one wooden trunk, and many pieces of junk and old furniture. The whole place was cramped and lonely and full of cool drafts, which were downright cold when the wind blew. He quickly stepped into his slippers and stomped his feet to get warm.

He had slept comfortably under the heavy pile of old quilts and blankets during the night. But as he hurriedly put on his clothes in the cool attic air, he bitterly remembered why the attic was now his new room for the indefinite future—Cousin Lester Laws and his son, Lester, Jr., had come to stay with the Kramars. Cousin Lester and Lester, Jr., had been given John's old room and John had been assigned to the attic. John felt as if he had been exiled to some strange, faraway land so he could freeze to death while distant relatives took over his room. He sighed as he pulled on his sweater.

John, eleven years old, was a normal boy with a slightly unusual background. When he was very young, his parents had disappeared in a terrible storm and were assumed dead. Ever since that time, John had lived with his Aunt Betty and Uncle Bill Kramar and their children, Susan, age thirteen, Lois, age eight, Katherine, who had just turned six years old—and now a new baby, Paul Nathaniel. After being with them so many years, he felt just like one of the family, but on that morning he began to wonder.

"I bet my real mom and dad wouldn't send me up here to freeze just because some stupid cousins came to visit," the boy muttered. "Why couldn't Cousin Lester and his bratty son sleep up here? Or the girls? Why is it always me who gets the bad deal?"

His aunt and uncle had been apologetic and explained several times why John was the natural one to sleep in the attic. Deep down, he knew they were probably right. Still, the whole thing made him mad. If it had been anyone else besides Cousin Lester and Lester, Jr., John wouldn't have cared so much.

Cousin Lester was a tall thin man, who wore wire-rim glasses with thick lenses. He was bald except for two patches of short gray hair on the sides of his head. He had a long, thin nose which he seemed to look down and aim at you like a gun whenever he looked your way, John thought. His thin bony face was wrinkled in a permanently disgusted expression, as if he had been sucking on a sour pickle for the last ten years. He had complained impatiently the whole time he had moved his things into John's old room.

"This room is hardly big enough for a grown man and a twelve-year-old boy," Cousin Lester had said as he dropped his bulky suitcase down on John's bed.

"It's the best we can do," Aunt Betty had replied. Cousin Lester was from her side of the family. He was at least ten years older than Betty. He was an accountant by profession, but had lost his job and much of his retirement when the company he'd worked for had gone bankrupt. His ex-wife lived far away in another state and had had little contact with them since the divorce, five years before.

"I guess we'll have to put up with it, until better arrangements can be made," Cousin Lester had grunted. Then he had stared at John. "How long is it going to take you to clear out that closet?"

"What a jerk!" John muttered. He looked around the attic, then he began to make his bed. He was just about to pull up the pile of blankets and quilts when he saw them. There on his pillow, was a large golden key ring, with several gold-colored keys, shimmering in the dim morning light that came in through the attic window. The boy stared at the strange keys in surprise. He was sure they hadn't been there a second ago. The keys almost seemed to move as they glistened, as if they were alive. What a silly idea, the boy thought. How could a key be alive? John reached down to touch them when fear suddenly gripped him.

Out of nowhere, a twinge of pain on the back of his neck distracted the boy. Instead of grabbing the keys, he reached up and rubbed his neck. A sense of gloom seemed to creep over him like a shadow. The keys grew dim, and in the blink of an eye, they disappeared like a mirage. John rubbed his eyes. He was sure he had seen them. Though the keys were gone, it seemed as if something or someone was in the attic with him. John whirled around. Everything looked the same. He felt foolish. He turned back to the bed. He pulled the blankets and quilt up over the pillow and walked quickly for the stairs.

John went down to the kitchen. He was all set to complain about having to sleep in the attic, but Cousin Lester was sitting at the table, drinking a cup of coffee and reading the newspaper. He frowned when he saw John.

"When are you going to move the rest of your stuff out of our room?" Cousin Lester asked as he glanced up at John. "I can hardly unpack my suitcase with the drawers all full of your things."

"Yeah, it's really crowded in there," Lester, Jr., added in his whining voice. Lester, Jr., sat beside his father, reading a comic book as he ate a bowl of cold cereal. John realized it was his own comic book just as Lester, Jr., dribbled milk on the open page.

"My comic book!" John cried out. He lunged forward to grab it, but Lester, Jr., pulled it out of John's reach.

"He made me do it," Lester, Jr., accused. "You saw it, Daddy."

"Why don't you go clean out your room instead of making messes down here?" Cousin Lester demanded.

John felt his face getting red. He was about to say a few choice words when Aunt Betty came into the kitchen.

"There you are," she said. "I thought you were out in the workshop. Before you go into town this morning, Cousin Lester would like you to clean out the drawers in your room. You can put your stuff in the dresser in the attic."

14

"Can't I do it after I come back from town?" John asked. "Mrs. Penn is only at the library a few hours this morning. I won't be able to get any books if I don't get there on time."

"You'll have time," Aunt Betty said. "What do you want for breakfast?"

"I'm not hungry," John said flatly. He looked at the table. Both Lesters were blissfully eating and reading. John left the room.

Thirty minutes later, he had cleared all his clothes from the closet and his old chest of drawers. He had also taken all his comic books and other choice possessions, hoping Lester, Jr., wouldn't notice. John put these in the old wooden trunk behind the dresser. The trunk's lock was broken, so John covered it with an old blanket, so no one would notice it.

"This room is still too small for a grown man and boy," Cousin Lester said as he unpacked his suitcase. John said nothing as he carried another box to the attic. He put the box on the floor by the dresser, then ran downstairs, going out the kitchen door.

John was glad to be outside, even though the day was damp and chilly. Gray clouds covered up the April sky and threatened rain. John hurried over to a long low building with large blue doors which was the farm's workshop. He opened one large blue door and went inside. He could hear voices in the next room.

John smiled for the first time that morning when he saw his Grandfather Kramar standing by a long workbench. Susan, Lois and Katherine Kramar were standing next to their grandfather, watching him as he worked on an old cuckoo clock. Normally his grandfather was up at his own farm. But since John's Uncle Bill was new at farming, Grandfather had come down to help out for a few weeks. While he was gone, Great Aunt Thelma was keeping Grandma Kramar company.

"That should make the cuckoo sing again," Grandfather said, running his hand through his white hair. He turned and smiled when he saw John. "Did you have a good night in the attic, my boy?"

"Are you kidding?" John asked. "It's freezing up there. The place is filled with junk, and it's dark and gloomy and lonely."

15

"You better get used to it," Susan Kramar said. "I heard Mom talking to Dad. They acted like Cousin Lester will be here for a while."

"Really?" John asked. He sighed loudly. "Why does he have to stay with us?"

"Because he's family and times are hard," Grandfather Kramar said as he turned back to the workbench. He picked up a tiny oil can. He carefully put a drop of oil on a large gear inside the clock. "When times are hard, we help out our friends and neighbors. And relatives, even if they aren't the ones we'd prefer to help. Like the Kings say, we are our brother's keeper. Besides, it won't last forever."

"How do we know that?" John demanded. "He's only been here a few days, and it already seems like forever. Besides, I don't think things are going to get better very soon with all the people in ORDER in power."

No one said anything for a moment. Everyone's life had changed since the Halloween War which had happened last October 31. The Halloween War had been one of the shortest, yet most destructive wars in history. The war had triggered all sorts of other problems, especially in the economies of countries all over the world. Every nation had been dramatically affected by what they called the Third Great Depression. Thousands of businesses and people went bankrupt. John didn't understand why it had happened so quickly. Life had been relatively peaceful and normal in Centerville a year ago. But so much had changed since then.

After the war, there had been a lot of confusion and fear. The television news had shown report after report of large gangs looting stores and stealing from people. Government elections had been delayed and emergency martial law went into effect all over the country. The ORDER political party, promising peace and safety and dramatic change, had influenced more and more people with its promises. When elections were finally held, the ORDER candidates had won all over the country and around the world. They proclaimed a new age of peace and safety and world order.

Because Uncle Bill Kramar was not a part of the ORDER political party, he had lost his job as sheriff of Centerville in the last election in December. Not long after that, the Kramar family had decided to move out to the farmhouse, which was eight miles to the west of town. Like most people, they were uncertain of what all the changes meant for their future. Uncle Bill had decided to work the farm and put in crops with Grandfather Kramar's help. Since the Kramars had sold their house in town, they had money in the bank to hold them over, but they weren't sure how long the money would last.

Since the election, things had settled down. There was less violence in the cities because there were many more ORDER security guards working with local and federal law officers. But other changes were coming. On January 1, New Year's Day, the government had announced a dramatic new step to deal with problems in the economy. They decreed that the whole economy, including local and federal banks, would officially shift over to the Point System on what they were calling Number Day, April 19. On that day, which also happened to be Easter Sunday, a person would no longer be able to use cash money to buy or sell anything. All buying and selling would have to be done with number cards.

The people in ORDER claimed that this would greatly reduce most crime and cheating. Most people were robbed for cash. Illegal drugs were also sold and bought with cash. But if the cash was no good, that would eliminate many problems. And since all goods and services would have to be paid for with a number card, the government computers could tell almost instantly who was buying what, when, where and for what price. All transactions could be traced and monitored. If people wanted to buy something, they had to have credit at the bank. The number cards and the Point System would keep track of everything automatically.

In the first week of January of that year, every person in the world was assigned a new number card. Everyone was instructed to turn in all cash for credit at their local banks as soon as possible. Cash could be used up to Number Day, but after that, it would be worthless. Most people began turning in their cash right away since they got bonus points for doing it early.

But not everyone thought the number cards or Number Day was a good idea. Lots of people, including the Kramar family, resisted using number cards. Though the number cards seemed to solve some problems, they also caused problems. Many people thought the number cards invaded their personal privacy for no reason. Others thought the Point System was unfair and that it gave the government too much control.

"I think things are going to get a lot worse before they get better," John said glumly to his cousins and grandfather. "I never would have thought things could change so much. I wish I'd never heard of number cards or ORDER. Or Cousin Lester."

"Maybe he'll act better once he feels settled in," Susan said sympathetically. "They've gone through a real hard time."

John looked at his watch and shook his head in dismay. He ran for an old red bicycle leaning near the door.

"I have to get into town while Mrs. Penn is still at the library," John said. "I'll see you later."

John pushed his old red bicycle out of the workshop. The bike rolled on big balloon tires. An old cracked mirror, a rubber horn and gear lever were attached to the handlebars. On the bar between the seat and handlebars, written in flowing white letters, were the words *Spirit Flyer*. Right below the handlebars, three golden crowns were linked together. Just as he was about to hop on, he saw them again. The golden keys and key ring were hanging on the handlebars. John stared at the keys.

"Maybe these are from the Three Kings," the boy said softly. "But what are they for?"

Just then, Cousin Lester came out of the house and stood on the

18

porch. He looked over at John. John felt a rush of anger. He pushed the old bicycle forward and hopped on. As he pedaled down the driveway, he heard Cousin Lester shout. John stood up on his pedals to go faster. He acted as if he didn't hear Cousin Lester.

"I'm not doing anything else for that old goat this morning," John muttered. As he turned out of the driveway onto Glory Road, he remembered the golden keys. He had forgotten about them as he made his escape. He looked down at the handlebars, but the keys were gone. John frowned. He was sure he had seen them. As he went over a bump in the road, he heard a small jangling sound, just like the sound of keys on a key ring. John frowned again, staring down at the handlebars.

Once again he felt as if someone was watching him. He pushed the unsettling feeling out of his mind as he began to pedal faster down the country road.

THE GARBAGE LADY

2

John headed for town. The boy looked straight ahead as he pedaled down the asphalt road. He pushed down on the handlebars of the old red Spirit Flyer. Without a sound, the front tire of the old red bicycle rose up into the air. A few seconds later, the back tire left the asphalt as the bike pulled away from the ground.

John began to pedal faster as he flew higher on the Spirit Flyer. He zipped up over the treetops. No matter how bad a mood he was in, it was always a thrill to clear the treetops, looking down at their branches. Most people in Centerville did not have Spirit Flyers or even believe that they could fly. But John knew they did, and it lifted his spirit.

He headed up to the clouds and pointed the Spirit Flyer toward Centerville. John would have gone higher, but the clouds were hanging heavy in the sky that day and he didn't feel like going through their damp mists. He glanced at his watch. He didn't have much time if he wanted to get to the library before it was too late. John stood up on the pedals to go faster. The wheels on the old bicycle hummed as he sped through the sky.

In a few moments he passed over the Sleepy Eye River near the outskirts of Centerville. John guided the old red bicycle downward. The Spirit Flyer touched down just outside of the town limits on Crofts Road.

He frowned as he rode the old red bicycle down the familiar Centerville streets. He rode over to Buckingham Street to Amy Burke's house. Amy and another friend, Daniel Bayley, were waiting outside. They smiled when John rode up.

"We thought you weren't coming in today," Daniel said. He had redder hair and more freckles than anybody John had ever known. Though Daniel had only lived in Centerville since August, he had become one of John's best friends.

"I wasn't sure I'd make it myself," John said, breathing hard. "My aunt's Cousin Lester and his son moved into our house a few days ago."

"Sounds crowded," Amy Burke said. Her hazel eyes twinkled.

"Cousin Lester is the reason I'm late," John said bitterly. "We better get to the library before Mrs. Penn leaves."

John pedaled down the street. Daniel and Amy rode beside him on their bicycles. Both Daniel and Amy rode old red Spirit Flyer bikes also. John was glad it was a Saturday because Amy and Daniel were off from school that day. John and the other Kramar kids had been going to school at home since January. John liked home schooling, but he did miss seeing some of his old friends like Daniel and Amy. Aunt Betty was a good teacher, and as it turned out, all the Kramar kids seemed to be learning more and faster while working at home. But John had other things on his mind than school that morning.

"It's not fair," John said with disgust as they turned onto Main Street and headed toward the town square. He rode slowly down the street. "None of this is fair."

"What's not fair?" Daniel asked.

"I feel like I'm being crowded out of everything," John said wearily. "We had to move out of Centerville, and now I've had to move out of my own room."

"You moved out?" Amy asked.

"I got kicked out," John replied. "Cousin Lester and his son, Lester, Jr., are staying in my room."

"I'd be upset too if I got kicked out of my room," Amy said.

"Centerville used to be a good place to live," John said with a sigh. "Now I feel like a stranger here, and I've lived here my whole life. I'm tired of being called names. I don't see why we should be singled out and made fun of just because we have Spirit Flyers and like the Kingson. Why should we have to use number cards if we don't like them? This used to be the land of the free . . . whatever happened to that freedom? Those ORDER people have ruined everything."

"Anyone who doesn't love ORDER is automatically an outsider," Daniel said. "If you're not with them, you're against them. That's just the way it is right now."

"Most people in town seem to like ORDER," Amy said. "They won the last elections here and all over the country."

"They're the majority all over the world now," Daniel added. "And the majority rules, even if it's fifty-one per cent to forty-nine per cent. But they say ORDER won by a landslide everywhere, if you can believe them."

"It doesn't make them right, even if they are the majority," John replied. "I think they're a bunch of creeps and sooner or later this town will wise up and see what a mistake they made in trusting them. I still say it's not fair."

As they got closer to the town square, John's bicycle slowed down and stopped. He frowned as he looked down.

"What's wrong?" Amy asked, pushing back on her brake. Daniel stopped beside her.

"I don't know," John said. "The bike just stopped."

He pushed on the pedals, but the wheels wouldn't turn. He was about to push harder when the big bike suddenly jerked forward and began rolling.

"It's going by itself," John said. He was only surprised for a few seconds. From experience, he knew that Spirit Flyers often took off in directions of their own. Normally, he was excited when the old bicycles chose their own new path because that meant they might be starting off on a new adventure. But that day he was frustrated and didn't feel in the mood to do anything other than what he had planned. He jerked the handlebars back in the original direction toward the library.

"Not now, you stupid bike," John moaned. "We have to get to the library before Mrs. Penn goes off duty, or we won't get any library books."

The other children watched John struggling to turn the handlebars. The old bike was moving so slowly that it seemed to be stuck in a mud hole.

"Maybe you should just ride it out," Daniel said as he watched his friend struggle.

"But we *have* to get to the library," John insisted, groaning as he jerked the handlebars once more.

"I think Daniel's right," Amy said. "You should let it take you where it wants. It might be more interesting than going to the library anyway."

John gave the handlebars one more wrenching jerk, then let go. He sat on the seat looking down at the old bike in disgust. He looked at his watch.

"Ok, then," he said to the others and to the bike. "Let's get this over with. Maybe we can still get to the library on time."

As soon as John took hold of the handlebars, the old red bicycle began rolling once again. The other children followed. John's Spirit Flyer headed east down Fourteenth Street and picked up speed. The three bikes and riders zipped along the old familiar streets of Centerville. John was surprised when the bike turned the corner and then stopped.

"It's your old house," Daniel said. "Why did the bicycle bring you here?"

"I don't know," John replied. He stared at the house. "The place is empty. Uncle Bill sold it, and now the people he sold it to are trying to sell it."

A blue and white For Sale sign was stuck in the front lawn. The empty house made John feel sad, then angry all over again. He spat on the ground.

"We wouldn't have had to move if it weren't for those jerks from ORDER," John spat out. "I lived in that house for years, ever since I can remember almost . . . ever since my parents died . . ."

John was silent, brooding inside. He tried to remember when he had moved into the old house, but couldn't. In an instant, a wave of sadness swept over the boy. He didn't want to think about it because he knew it had to do with the loss of his parents.

"Why do you think your bike brought you here?" Daniel asked.

"Who knows?" John answered. He felt a surge of anger cover the sadness. He looked around. The street looked the same, though two other houses were also up for sale. The Carsons and the Willoughbys had both moved that winter because they had lost their jobs. Both of them had been opposed to ORDER also.

Just then, a woman turned the corner and walked up the sidewalk. John stared at her. The first thing he noticed was that she wasn't wearing any shoes even though the weather was chilly. Her clothes, a pair of black pants and a scarlet blouse, looked as if they had been expensive once, but were now worn and ragged. Her dirty hair was a mess and covered half her face. She walked unsteadily down the sidewalk, pausing to look at the houses. She muttered softly to herself, then coughed. The children all stared at her. As she came closer, they moved their bikes off the sidewalk so she could pass.

But instead of walking past them, she stopped. She stared at John's old house for a long time. Then she squinted at the number above the mailbox.

"Do you know her?" Amy asked John softly.

"Are you kidding?" John whispered. Something about the woman's strange appearance made him feel uneasy. "She looks like she escaped from a loony bin or something. Do you see the dirt on her hands and feet?"

"Shsshh! She'll hear you," Amy said.

The woman turned around and looked at the For Sale sign in the front yard. She pushed back her dirty hair with her hand. She coughed loudly again. She walked up to the front steps.

"The people that used to live here moved last December," Amy called out to the woman. She stared at the children, but her eyes seemed unfocused, as if she didn't see them. She sat down on the steps, looking at the sign.

"I wonder if she needs help," Amy asked.

"I doubt if she could buy a house," John said. "I think she must be lost. Or maybe she did escape from jail or something."

"She'll hear you," Amy whispered.

The woman stood up unsteadily. She stared at the children once more. She walked over to the sign in the middle of the yard. She touched the painted letters. She turned and began to walk back in the direction she had come. The children watched quietly until she turned the corner.

"What a weirdo," John said. Then he looked at his watch. "Maybe if we hurry we can get to the library on time, if this bike will go in the right direction."

John turned his big Spirit Flyer bike around. He was relieved that the old bike didn't resist him when he began to pedal.

John raced toward the town library. Daniel and Amy were right behind him. John rode on the other side of the street as they passed the strange barefoot woman. But as he passed her, his bike began to wobble. John gripped the handlebars tighter and pedaled faster. The wobble seemed to disappear after they reached the corner.

The children parked their bikes at the rack under the big oak tree by the library. John raced up the steps and was the first one in the door. His face fell when he saw Ms. Wadpoole behind the checkout desk. Ms. Wadpoole was the new librarian. She stared up at John and then looked back down at her desk.

"Is Mrs. Penn still here?" John asked.

"She's gone for the day," Ms. Wadpoole said. "She's only here part of the morning on Saturdays. May I help you?"

"No, thanks," John said.

Daniel was already looking at the shelves of science books. John sighed. He didn't think it was any use. Daniel took three volumes off the shelves and walked over to the checkout counter.

"Your number card, please," Ms. Wadpoole asked.

"I have my old library card," Daniel said. He took out an orange card. He handed it to the librarian.

"I'm sorry," Ms. Wadpoole said. "You must not know the new rules. You must have a current number card to check out books. So if you let me have your number card, I will check you out."

"I don't have a number card," Daniel said firmly.

"You don't have a number card?" Ms. Wadpoole asked. She seemed surprised. Then she looked at Daniel, John and Amy carefully. She took off her glasses and began to clean them with a tissue. "You children must be aware of the rules. No number card, no check out. The library has had signs posted stating that for several weeks now. Like everyone else, we've shifted over to the Point System."

"But we're citizens of this town and county," Amy said. "Our families pay taxes. We deserve to get books like everyone else."

"Then you should get your number cards like everyone else, and then you can check out books like everyone else," Ms. Wadpoole said. "You can go right down the street and get your number card at the court-house. Then you can check out all the books you want."

A boy and his mother walked up behind Daniel holding books. Daniel moved to one side. The boy, a first grader named Elwin Brooks, gave Ms. Wadpoole a stack of ten books. She smiled sweetly. She picked up a number probe, which was a pen-shaped instrument. She passed the tip of the number probe over the code number on the back of each book.

"May I have your number card, Elwin?"

The little boy handed the librarian a rectangular piece of black plastic about the size of a credit card. A row of purple numbers blinked on and off on the number card. Ms. Wadpoole stuck the card into a slot on a black panel directly behind her desk. The four-inch-thick panel was three feet wide and one foot tall.

The black panel flashed a series of numbers and letters. Then words appeared. "Elwin Brooks Approved!"

John stared at the black panel with disgust. On the front was the name, *Big Board—Point Panel, Jr.* For a moment, John wished he had a hammer so he could break the Big Board. But he knew it wouldn't do any good. Big Boards of all types and sizes were everywhere in Centerville now. Many people even had them in their homes, even though they were quite expensive. Most people thought they needed them since the power and the influence of the Point System had spread. Pretty soon, they'd be as common as TVs and telephones, John thought.

The Point System was the reason Big Boards and number cards existed. Everything about a person or a group or a business was broken down into points. The Big Boards, which were all on a network together, kept track of these points for the Point System. To John it had seemed like a kind of report card at first, only much bigger. The Big Board not only kept track of student's grades and scores on tests, but it also kept track of almost everything you could imagine—from I.Q. points to grade points to good and bad points to overall personality points and popularity points. Then those points, negative and positive, were all added up to form a person's overall point total or score. The higher your overall point total, the better your rank. And the better your rank, the more everyone thought of you.

But now the Point System had gotten worse, John thought. All businesses used the Big Boards, the schools used Big Boards, and government offices used them too. Even the library had shifted over. Every where you looked, signs and billboards announced: "The Point System—The Only Game in Town."

But not everyone wanted to play along with the Point System rules. John and his family and many people in Centerville had refused to go along with the Point System. They just didn't use the little black number cards. But anyone who refused to go by Point System rules was officially labeled a Rank Blank. As the Point System spread, it divided the town of Centerville into two camps. The majority of the town went under the Point System authority, while the minority refused. After the ORDER political party won the election, the government had transferred all record keeping over to the Point System. And since the government had announced that Number Day was coming and all banks would be on the Point System, it seemed as if the Point System was destined to take over everyone's life. John didn't see how they could keep resisting. If you had to have a number card if you wanted to buy food, how could you refuse?

"You children know the rules," Ms. Wadpoole said crisply. "I remember your names. I shall have to report this incident to the library board."

The children left the library slowly. John frowned all the way to the bicycle racks. He knocked the kickstand up angrily with his foot.

"I told you we would be late," he said. "We could have had books from Mrs. Penn if this stupid old bike hadn't taken us off on some wild goose chase."

"I don't think it's fair either," Daniel said as they rode into the Centerville town square. "I suppose I could get my sister to get us some books. She has a number card."

"That might work," Amy agreed.

A noise caught the children's attention. Down the block, inside the town square near the old gazebo, a group of boys in gray uniforms were laughing and shouting.

"That's Sloan Favor and his friends," Daniel said.

"What are they doing?" John asked sourly. Before anyone could answer, John's old red bicycle shot forward. John leaned backward. Daniel and Amy's bikes also shot forward. They headed straight across the street toward Sloan and the group of boys.

As they got closer, John saw the same strange-looking woman that had stopped at his old house. She was next to the old town well. The well had been bricked up years ago, but a drinking fountain and a faucet stuck out of the side of the bricks. The boys in gray uniforms had formed a circle around her. A garbage container was tipped over with paper and trash strewn all over the ground. The boys were wadding up pieces of the trash and throwing them at the woman, shouting and laughing.

"Garbage Lady, Garbage Lady!" they called, pelting the woman. She turned in confused circles, trying to duck and avoid the wads of paper.

John tried to brake his old bicycle, but the Spirit Flyer only seemed to go faster, straight for the gang of boys tormenting the woman.

When Sloan saw the three bicycles heading straight for them, his eyes grew wide with surprise. The gang of boys yelled out in fear when they realized the bicycles showed no signs of stopping!

ORDER
AT THE
DUMP
· · · · · · · ·

The boys in the gray uniforms jumped out
of the way as the big red bicycles shot between them and the woman.
Sloan Favor was so startled that he tripped backward over a small bush
as he tried to get out of the way. He scrambled back to his feet, a large
scowl on his face.

"Who are you trying to run over with those stupid bikes?" Sloan
demanded angrily. "You don't have any right to run us down."

"And you don't have any right to bother this woman," Daniel Bayley
replied firmly. He too was surprised the Spirit Flyers had charged into
the crowd of boys. But deep down, he knew there must be a reason.

The woman stared fearfully at all the children. She held an empty plastic milk jug. Water ran out of a small faucet that was connected to a drinking fountain. Sloan walked over and turned off the water.

"This woman was stealing town water!" Sloan announced as he turned off the squeaky faucet handle.

"She can have that water if she wants," John Kramar said. "Anyone can get water out of there. You're just trying to give her a hard time."

"We're part of the Commando Street Patrol, and we can stop bums like this Garbage Lady from stinking up this town," Sloan replied. "She doesn't live here. We asked her. She doesn't belong here, and we aren't going to let her drink town water. We don't want trash like her cluttering up our clean streets."

"There is a lot of trash loose on the streets these days," Amy Burke said as she stared at the group of boys in the gray uniforms. Sloan took a step toward Amy but then stopped.

"You're lucky you're a girl," Sloan said, spitting on the ground. "I might have known you Rank Blanks would try to protect suspicious characters like this Garbage Lady. All this is going down in my report."

Sloan took a small black notebook out of his back pocket. He flipped open the pages and began writing. The other boys in the group smiled triumphantly. John watched the strange woman. She brushed her scraggly hair away from her face. She held the empty jug tightly. John noticed that her arms were shaking and trembling.

John walked over and took the jug gently from her hands. He bent down, turned on the water faucet, and held the jug underneath it.

"I'm filling this with water and you can write that down in your little book too," John said defiantly.

"You can bet I will," Sloan said as he continued to write. "I don't know why you losers should stick up for this Garbage Lady. I guess losers like to stick with other losers."

The gang of boys began laughing. The woman shivered in the afternoon air. When the jug was full, John turned off the water. He handed it to the woman. She seemed so frail that she could hardly hold it.

"Maybe you should pour some of the water out so it won't be so heavy," Amy said and stepped forward. "I'll help you."

The strange woman clutched the jug tighter, as if she was afraid to lose it a second time. Amy stepped back.

"You can keep it," Daniel said softly, trying to reassure the frightened woman. "We won't hurt you."

"She's a nut case," Sloan said in disgust. He finished writing in his little black notebook. He closed it and put it into his back pocket. "I'll be letting the people in ORDER and the town sheriff know we've got a crazy woman on the loose here in Centerville. They've been watching those Garbage People out at the dump for some time. They're going to clean up that place, sooner than you think."

"You don't know that she lives out there," Daniel said. The woman began to back away, carrying her jug of water. She walked across the street and then headed south down the alley.

"She looks crazy to me," Roger Darrow said. He wore a gray uniform like the other boys.

"You used to be a friend," John said, looking at Roger sadly. Roger looked away uneasily as John stared at him. Roger was a boy who had resisted the Point System at first, but then gave up to follow the crowd.

"Roger wised up," a Commando named Jason said. "He knows who's important in this town."

"Yeah, he knows who's Number One around here," Sloan said. The blond boy smiled at his friends. He took a black plastic number card out of his pocket and held it up for the others to see. A large purple *Number 1: Children's Division* flashed on and off. "Let's leave these losers alone. The stink is beginning to make my stomach hurt."

The boys in the gray uniforms laughed as they picked up their bicycles. Making jokes among themselves, they rode slowly out into the street. John shook his head as he watched them ride away.

"They get all kinds of special privileges as ORDER Commandos," John said bitterly, "and we can't even check out library books."

"I better go get my shoes," Daniel said. "I told my mom I would do it today."

The three children hopped on their bikes once more. They pedaled out of the town square and went down Main Street. John was bitter all over again as they passed the library. When they reached Carson's Shoe Store, they hopped off their bikes.

Daniel picked out a pair of shoes and tried them on. They fit. He carried the box up to the counter by the door.

"Daniel, my favorite red-headed customer," Mr. Carson said with a smile. He was a short, old man with a big gray mustache. His spoke with a slight accent because he was originally from Italy. Daniel smiled as he counted out the money and put it on the counter.

"Cash, eh?" Mr. Carson said. He stroked the mustache. "You're one of the few people using cash money anymore. I guess it won't be long before those government folks come in and take out the cash register altogether. That's the new rules. I won't need it since no one will have cash. We'll all be using number cards. You won't be able to buy anything without those cards, they say."

"Number Day isn't far off," Daniel replied, nodding his head. "They say they're switching over to stop crime and to stop people from cheating on their taxes, but I think they just want to control everyone."

"Well, I won't be getting any more bad checks," Mr. Carson said. "With those number cards, you either have the money in the bank, or you can't buy it. My little Point Register lets you know the situation right away."

Mr. Carson patted a long black box sitting next to the old cash register. A woman came up to the counter behind Daniel. The children backed away as the woman handed Mr. Carson her number card. He put the card in the slot in the top of the box and passed the shoe boxes over the code reader. The amounts flashed on the Point Register in purple letters. The dark box seemed to hum for an instant. Then a number appeared, followed by the word *Approved.* Mr. Carson took out the number card and gave it to the woman. She smiled and left the store.

"Now that's an easy, safe way to do business," Mr. Carson said. "Had a man in here this morning. Rough-looking character. I think he was from that gang living out by the dump. He tried to get some work boots. But his card wasn't approved. Now in the old days, if I had taken a check from that bum, I would have never seen my shoes again or any money. These cards sure are an easy way to do business."

"Yeah," Daniel said glumly. "But what about the people who don't want to use those cards? What will happen to us?"

"I don't know," Mr. Carson said slowly, rubbing his mustache. "I guess we'll have to wait and see. You children be good, now."

The old man picked up a broom and began to sweep.

Daniel opened the front door and went outside, followed by John and Amy.

John sighed as he got on his bike. "I think this whole situation is going to get a lot worse before it gets better," John said sadly. "If it does get better."

"Why don't you come to my house?" Daniel said. "I still have lots of books you haven't read. You can borrow some of mine."

John and Amy nodded. The children rode silently side by side to Daniel's house. An hour later, John came back outside with two books under his arm. He strapped the books onto the back of his bike and then hopped on.

The sky was getting darker. John frowned. The heavy gray clouds seemed to be just like the boy's bad mood. He pedaled the old red bicycle quickly down the Centerville streets, glancing up at swirling clouds. He turned onto Cemetery Road. The big Goliath Industries factory was belching thick black smoke into the sky. He passed the cemetery and the ORDER Security Center. A guard at the gate watched as John pedaled by.

The boy pedaled slowly, lost in his thoughts. Then he looked down at his watch. With a sigh, he pushed down on his handlebars so they pointed upward. The big balloon tires left the ground and the old red bike rose into the air. The wheels made a soft hum as they turned.

John shot up into the sky. He cleared the treetops, and sped beneath the clouds. He turned the Spirit Flyer toward the family farm.

Suddenly, the bike turned to the left. John sat back down and got a better grip on the handlebars. He turned the bike in its original direction. But as soon as he was headed for home, the bicycle swerved again and headed south.

"What's wrong with you today?" John asked with frustration. As if to answer, the old red bicycle shot forward in the sky, going south.

John held on tightly, wondering where the bike was taking him. He zoomed silently through the air. The only sound was the soft humming of the spinning wheels. The boy and bike sped over the forest below. John looked at the town of Centerville off to his left. The angry clouds blowing in from the west made the boy nervous. The clouds looked full of rain and lightning.

Finally the old red bicycle began to descend. John was right over a small dirt road that led out to the town dump. Mounds of garbage filled the dump like small mountains. As the bicycle dropped closer to the ground, the blowing wind carried the stinks and smells upward. The smells were particularly bad that day, John thought.

As the bike got closer, John saw them. Several jeeps and trucks were parked on the road. He thought he heard a scream above the noise of trucks moving. The boy began to feel afraid.

From behind a mound of garbage, two large gray trucks rolled into view. Instead of tires, the trucks had big tracks, like bulldozers. A metal turret with a long barrel was sticking out on top of each truck. The vehicles looked something like tanks. John had seen them before on TV news. They were also parked out at the ORDER Security Center. They were called Riot Trucks by the newscasters. A white circle with a white X inside it was painted on the sides of the big vehicles. The circled white X was on all official ORDER equipment.

The large trucks rolled slowly forward toward a row of little shacks made out of cardboard, tin, old furniture and other kinds of junk at the far north end of the dump. They were the homes of the Garbage People, as the town called them. John had seen the little shacks before. He even knew the names of many of the people. The Kramar family and several other people with Spirit Flyers had gone to the dump each week since late February. Each time they had talked with the people and given them sacks of groceries and clothes. Every week John had seen more shacks and new faces. His uncle had said the little makeshift towns were common in most communities ever since the war.

John had seen stories about the little towns on television. In every story he had seen, the government accused the homeless people of all kinds of bad things. Often ORDER trucks were shown coming and destroying the little shacks.

John felt as if he were watching one of those same television reports as he looked down at the scene below, but this was really happening in the Centerville dump. As the Riot Trucks moved closer, the people began to run away. Just then, streams of dark gray water shot out of the barrels of the trucks. The water shot out with such force that when it hit the first shack, the walls blew apart like tissue paper. John's bike stopped in the sky. From up high, the people looked like insects running out from under an overturned rock. The Riot Trucks rolled forward, their water jets knocking down more shacks. They moved on, crushing the shacks beneath the heavy metal tracks. The stream of water shot out after the people who were running away. John saw several men, women and children knocked off their feet as the water hit them.

John recognized the woman he had seen in town because of her scarlet blouse. She was trotting, very unsteadily, down the old dump road. The bicycle shot forward and dropped lower at the same time as it moved toward the dump. The air was filled with loud cries. John dropped below the trees and couldn't see anything for a moment. When

he was right above the dump road, he saw the woman again. She was about a hundred yards down the road, still trotting, holding her water jug. A man in a gray uniform was chasing her. Suddenly, the old red Spirit Flyer seemed to leap forward. The bike zoomed over the road, two feet off the ground. John passed the man in the gray uniform easily. The old red bike passed the woman and then landed softly.

The woman stopped and stared at John. She was soaking wet, her bare feet muddy. She was shivering and holding onto the plastic jug, half filled with water.

"Get on," John said without thinking. The woman looked behind her. The man in the gray uniform was running faster. He shouted something. The woman turned back to John.

"Hop on the back and hold onto my waist," John said. The woman nodded. She quickly got on the back of the red bike. As soon she got on, the bicycle began to move. The woman held onto John's waist with one hand and the plastic milk jug with the other hand. John looked over his shoulder. The man in the gray uniform looked very angry. The old red bicycle rose into the air and quickly picked up speed. John aimed the handlebars up and the bike cleared the treetops. In a few moments, the dump was far behind them.

ANOTHER VISITOR ARRIVES

. . . .

4

A few minutes later, the bike began to slow down. John could feel the woman behind him shaking and shivering. Her wet clothes were getting him wet too.

John saw his house up ahead. He guided the bicycle down past the trees. The tires touched down softly, and the old red bike coasted to a stop where the driveway met the road.

The woman got off. She was still shivering. She stared at John and the bicycle with eyes full of fear. John didn't know if she was afraid of him or afraid about what had happened at the dump, or afraid of riding on the Spirit Flyer. The woman rubbed her wet arms. The water was still dripping off her.

"I'm cold," the woman said, rubbing her arms harder.

"I better take you home with me," John said. "My aunt and uncle will know what to do. That's our house, right up the driveway."

John pointed at a white house with blue trim. The woman stared at the house and then rubbed her eyes. She stared again at the house for a long time. Then she looked over at John.

"Where are we?" she asked.

"We're outside of Centerville about eight miles," John replied. "This is Glory Road."

"Glory Road?" she asked.

"Yes," John said. "Have you ever heard of it?"

The woman didn't answer. Her eyes suddenly seemed to be looking right through the boy. John felt uncomfortable.

"This is a farm on 10100 Glory Road," John said. "That's our house. Let's go up there. You could probably get some dry clothes. By the way, my name is John Kramar. I know my aunt has clothes that would—"

Just then, the woman jerked, then crumpled and fell to the ground. John ran over. The woman was still breathing, but she seemed asleep.

"She must have fainted," John thought. "Or maybe she's really sick!"

A wave of fear and panic passed over the boy like a shadow. The woman seemed very pale and fragile. Suddenly, rain began to fall. Thunder rumbled far off in the distance. He was about to run up to the house when he heard the sound of a motor. John looked up. The sound of the chugging was louder and right overhead. John waved frantically as a large red tractor pulling a hay wagon moved into view over the top of a large oak tree. The tractor circled in the air and glided downward. Grandfather Kramar was behind the wheel. The old red tractor, which had the name *Spirit Flyer Harvester* painted in white letters on the side, touched down and came to a halt.

"Grandfather Kramar!" John yelled. "There's a sick woman here! I was giving her a ride on my bike and then she fainted or something. She may be really sick."

Grandfather Kramar pushed the throttle down so the tractor chugged softly. Then he climbed down quickly from the broad metal seat. In a moment he was by John's side. The old man stared at the woman for a long moment with his mouth open but without speaking. John looked at his grandfather.

"What's wrong?" John asked. He could tell that something about the woman had surprised the old man.

Suddenly he seemed to come to himself and said, "We better get her up to the house." He touched the woman's neck. "Why is she so wet?"

"The ORDER Security Squad people sprayed all the people living out at the town dump with those Riot Trucks," John said. "They were knocking down all the huts they lived in and going after them. The Spirit Flyer led me to this woman. She was running away too. When I got here, she just fell over. Is she going to die?"

"I think she's just fainted," the old man said. "But we need to get her to the house. We can give her dry clothes and call Doc Brimberry."

John helped the old man carry the woman to the hay wagon. John held her head in his lap as his grandfather drove the tractor up to the house. Aunt Betty came out on the porch. When she saw the woman, she ran down the steps to help carry her in. Cousin Lester came out on the porch as they lifted her out of the wagon.

"My goodness, who is that woman?" Cousin Lester asked. "She is sopping wet!"

"John helped her escape the Riot Trucks out at the dump," Grandfather Kramar said.

"Let me help," Aunt Betty said. She grabbed the woman's feet. As she started up the steps, she looked into the woman's pale face, then stopped. "Oh, my! It can't be. I don't believe it." She quickly looked at Grandfather Kramar. The old man shrugged his shoulders. John watched his aunt and his grandfather.

"What's going on?" John asked. "Why do you guys look so funny? Do you know this woman?"

"Let's get her into the house," Grandfather Kramar said, and began moving up the steps again.

"Is this woman in some sort of trouble with the ORDER people?" Cousin Lester asked. He looked at the woman, crinkling his nose in distaste. "If she is, I don't know if we should get involved. She could bring trouble to us all by her staying here. I know what I'm talking about. Believe me, I've seen it. Those ORDER people can come in and cause a lot of trouble very quickly if you mess in their business."

"This woman needs help," Grandfather Kramar said. "Just like you needed help when you came here."

"Well, I'm sure she does need help," Cousin Lester said, following them down the hallway. "But I think you'd be wise to think it over. After all, I'm not in trouble with the police or with ORDER."

"Let's take her upstairs," Aunt Betty said. "We need to get her into some dry clothes."

"Upstairs?" Cousin Lester asked. "You aren't going to put her in my room, are you?"

Grandfather Kramar stopped. He turned and looked hard at Cousin Lester.

"I don't want to be unkind, but after all, it's already crowded enough in my room," Cousin Lester said. "With Les, Jr., in there, I hardly have room to turn around."

"We'll put her in our room, Lester," Aunt Betty said.

John followed them up the stairs. He opened the door to his aunt and uncle's bedroom. After they placed her on the bed, Grandfather Kramar led the boy out of the room.

"Your aunt can take care of things for now," the old man said. "Let's go call Doc Brimberry."

His grandfather made the call, then went downstairs to the kitchen. He put a fresh kettle of water on the stove.

"I think we could all use a nice cup of tea."

"What's wrong with that woman?" John asked. "Is she really sick?"

"I hope not," the old man said slowly. He didn't seem certain, which bothered the boy. His grandfather usually made everything seem as if there wouldn't be anything to worry about. But this time his grandfather seemed caught off guard, as if he was troubled. Cousin Lester came into the kitchen. His sour face looked more sour than usual.

"Where did you find that woman, anyway?" Cousin Lester asked.

"I was riding home and my Spirit Flyer took me out by the dump," John said. "The ORDER Riot Trucks were there, spraying people, knocking down their little huts and homes. They rolled over their shacks in those tank trucks. People were yelling and screaming as they ran away. She was running down the old dump road. My Spirit Flyer took me right to her. I knew I was supposed to give her a ride."

"How can you be sure, with those old bicycles?" Cousin Lester asked. "I have a Spirit Flyer bike, just like you, and I never rescued anybody with it."

"I'm not surprised at that," Grandfather Kramar said softly.

"You don't even ride your bike, do you?" John asked Cousin Lester.

"I've ridden it a few times," the tall thin man said. He grabbed a tissue off the table and blew his long nose. "But lately I've been more careful. You can get into a lot of trouble if people know you have those bicycles. I have a hard enough time as it is without complicating my life with those strange old bikes. I like the Kings as much as anyone in their kingdom, but I don't believe in sticking my neck out unnecessarily like you did, my boy."

"I had to give her a ride or the man chasing her would have caught her," John said.

"There was a man chasing her?" Cousin Lester asked. "You mean he saw you give her a ride?"

"He sure did," John said, almost with a smile. "I bet he's still scratching his head after seeing us take off."

"Oh, dear, I'm afraid this whole thing is going to mean trouble and

43

more trouble," Cousin Lester said. "She must have been breaking the law. We are harboring a fugitive from justice."

"Justice!" John burst out. "What kind of justice is it when ORDER tries to take over everybody's life in this town?" The teakettle began to boil. Uncle Bill came in through the kitchen door.

"I hear we have a visitor," Uncle Bill said seriously. Grandfather Kramar nodded. The two men left the room. Cousin Lester paced back and forth across the kitchen floor while John poured boiling water over a tea bag in a ceramic mug.

"Trouble, trouble, trouble," Cousin Lester said, shaking his head. "I don't see why my boy and I should be dragged into other people's problems. Especially the problems like those Garbage People out at the dump."

"Uncle Bill and Aunt Betty said we shouldn't call them those names," John said.

"Don't correct me, young man. I'm only repeating what they call them on the television," Cousin Lester said. "We had those same kind of people living in my old town too. They just caused trouble to ordinary decent citizens like myself."

John was about to reply when his uncle and grandfather came into the kitchen. Both men stared at John for a moment and then back at each other.

"Well, what's happened?" Cousin Lester asked. "Is the doctor coming? She didn't die, did she?"

"The doctor is coming," Grandfather Kramar said. "I don't know how sick she is, but she does seem rather upset and disturbed."

"You aren't telling me something," John said. He looked at his grandfather and uncle, who both looked uneasy. "Is there something else wrong?"

Grandfather Kramar made himself a cup of tea. He took a sip and stared out the window. He didn't seem to be listening to John.

"Do you know who she is?" John asked. "Why aren't you telling me what's going on?"

"He might as well know," Uncle Bill said.

"Know what?" John demanded.

"The woman upstairs," Grandfather Kramar said slowly, "is your mother."

MARY KRAMAR

• • • • • • • •

5

"My mother?" John asked. He dropped hard on a chair. For a moment, he almost felt sick. He took in great gulps of air as if he were having trouble breathing. The word *mother* echoed in his head over and over as his mind tried to understand it. Everything suddenly seemed so far away. John felt wave after wave of indescribable emotions washing over him. His thoughts raced in confusion. He was trying to understand that his mother was here, in the flesh, alive, after so many years.

"I don't know how to explain what's happened," Grandfather Kramar said. "I'm sure there's a reason, a story about what has gone on. But that's your mother upstairs. I'd know her anywhere. She's in sad shape, and she looks older than I would have imagined. But she's your mom. We asked her who she was and she told us: Mary Kramar. She has a birthmark behind her right ear in the shape of a bell just like your mother did."

"I don't believe it," John said, his voice cracking. "It has to be some kind of trick. Someone is trying to hurt me again."

The boy's eyes filled with tears. He shook his head from side to side. "That can't be her. She's dead."

Grandfather Kramar came over and put his big hand on John's shoulder. He patted him as John began to sob. Aunt Betty came into the room quietly. When she saw John, she knew that he had been told. She looked at Grandfather Kramar uncertainly. The old man said nothing. He continued to pat John on the back as the boy cried. John looked up with tears on his cheeks.

"I've got to go to her," John said suddenly. "I've got to go be with her. Maybe . . . maybe my father's alive too. Maybe she knows where he is."

John got out of his chair and raced up the stairs. He hit the bedroom door hard, knocking it open. The room was dark. The frail woman was lying on the bed. The window was open, and rain was still falling outside. John walked slowly over to her. He reached out and touched his mother's hand. She moaned in her sleep. Over the years he had imagined his mother and father coming home. He saw himself running and laughing into their arms. In his dreams, his parents hugged him forever it seemed, until all the lost empty feeling the boy held inside was soothed away. In their arms, everything suddenly made sense and there was a great peace. Once they were together as a family, John knew he would be home with nothing to be afraid of ever again. The whole dream seemed so right and pure and full of joy.

But this was different. John could hardly believe the sick woman lying on the bed in front of him was his mother. She seemed so distant and strange, not at all like he had imagined. She was too sick to hug him. There was no joy in her pale face.

Grandfather Kramar, Uncle Bill and Aunt Betty came into the room. They watched John quietly. His cheeks were wet as he looked at his mother.

"She seems to be very sick, John," Grandfather Kramar said.

"She seemed delirious to me," Cousin Lester said.

"But she'll get better, won't she?" John asked.

"We hope so," Aunt Betty said. "She probably needs to rest."

"But I've got to know what happened," John said anxiously. "I've got to know where she's been and why she stayed away so long. And I've got to know what happened to my father. She must know."

Aunt Betty and Uncle Bill looked uneasily at Grandfather Kramar. The old man rubbed his cheek as he stared at John and his mother.

"John, we're all in as much shock about this as you are and have just as many questions that we want answered. But your mother is weak, and we should let her sleep if she needs to rest," the old man said softly. John's mother opened her eyes at that moment. She stared up at John.

"It's me, John, your son," John said quickly. He wiped his face with the back of his arm. "You've come home and you're safe now."

"Where am I?" Mary Kramar asked, looking around the room.

"You're at 10100 Glory Road," John said. "You used to live here, remember? You and Dad lived on this farm. But Uncle Bill and Aunt Betty live here now. I'm John, your son."

"John's dead. They're all dead," the woman whispered. "They got us, all right. Everyone is gone. We'll have to make it on our own now."

"But I'm not dead," John said quickly. "I'm right here. I'm John. Your son."

The frail woman frowned as she looked at John. She didn't seem to recognize him. Grandfather walked over behind John.

"She seems to have come a long way," the old man said gently. "I think she needs time to get readjusted. It looks like she's been through

48

a lot. She's still confused."

"Can I have a Vitamin Z Shake?" John's mother asked. "Or maybe some Z-Pops. I always feel better after some Z-Pops. Please let me have some."

His mother's hands reached out, as if to receive some invisible gift. Her hands trembled as they hung in the air, waiting.

"What's a Z-Pop?" John asked. His uncle Bill frowned as he looked down on the woman.

"Where's Joe?" Uncle Bill asked. "Is Joe still alive?"

"Joe?" the old woman asked.

"Where's Joe Kramar?" Uncle Bill asked again. "Is he alive?"

"Joe's out calling the hogs," the exhausted woman said. "He's out calling the hogs like usual."

John's mother smiled, but it wasn't a happy smile. "He calls out the hogs every day. He's a pig himself. I've seen it. A dirty old pig."

"What's she talking about?" John asked. "Mother it's me, John. I'm your son. You've come home."

"There's no way home," his mother said sadly. She seemed to be looking right through him. "We did terrible things. We're just no good. We gave John up. Joe's brother adopted him. He's safe, now. It's OK because he's safe, and they won't get him. We gave him up. They said to, or else they would hurt him. They wanted to kill us all, but we gave him up . . ."

Aunt Betty took over a tray with a cup of tea and some cookies. John's mother sat up higher in the bed. She took the teacup with trembling hands and drank. John was surprised she could drink such hot tea so quickly. She ate a cookie off the plate, then another, chewing as if she were starved.

"What happened, Mary?" Grandfather Kramar asked. "What happened in that storm when you and Joe left?"

A look of terror crossed Mary Kramar's face. She frowned, as if trying to remember.

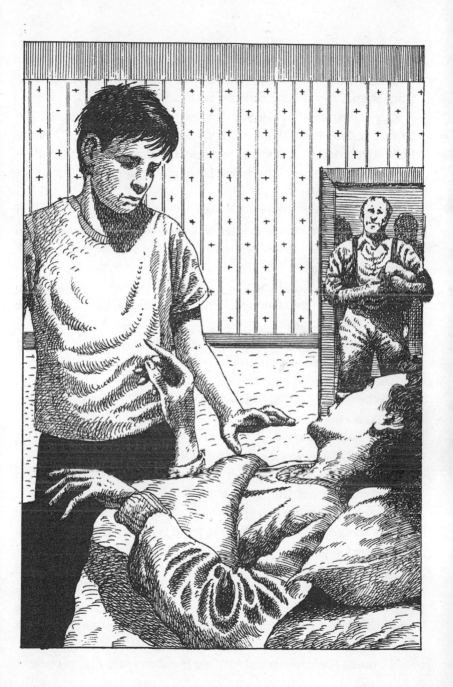

"Joe opened the toy store," Grandfather Kramar said. "You both had Spirit Flyers. Do you remember the storm and the tornado?"

Mary Kramar cringed back. She dropped the teacup on the saucer. The cup broke in half and the remaining tea spilled on the bed. "Not the snake!" she cried out. "Don't let him have the chain. Don't let him have the chain. I don't want it no more. Leave me be. All I want is a Z-Pop, can't I have it now . . ."

The woman kept jabbering for some minutes before she drifted off into restless sleep. She turned her head back and forth on the pillow, moaning loudly. She shook even more violently, as if trying to shake off some awful dream.

"Help her!" John said frantically. He ran to her side. She looked so distressed that he was afraid to touch her. "Mother, it's all right. You're home now."

Grandfather Kramar pulled John gently away as Aunt Betty put a wet washrag on his mother's forehead.

"She has a fever," Aunt Betty said.

"We better let your mother rest," Grandfather Kramar said, leading John toward the door.

"But I have to know what happened!" John cried out. "Is she going to be all right? Why was she gone for so long?"

"There'll be time," Grandfather Kramar said. "The doctor's here now. Let him examine her. Doc Brimberry will help her."

An older man came into the room carrying a small black bag. He looked serious. Grandfather Kramar led John out into the hall. Aunt Betty stayed in the room with the doctor. The door shut.

They seemed to take forever in the room, John thought as he paced across the old throw rug on the living room floor. Finally, Doctor Brimberry came out of the room. John jumped to his feet. The doctor frowned. He put his stethoscope and thermometer in his small black bag. He sat down on a chair in the hall and sighed.

"I wouldn't believe it possible," Doc Brimberry said. "I don't believe

I've seen your mother since the day she brought you in for a tetanus shot. I remember that because it was right before the long rain we had that year, the one with all the tornadoes. You remember, don't you, Bill?"

"Sure I do," Uncle Bill said. "Who could forget that time?"

"That's when my parents' car was found, right?" John asked. "Everyone thought they were dead. But my mom's alive. And maybe my father is too. She mentioned him."

"She did?" Doc Brimberry asked.

"Before you came, she said something about Joe and pigs," Bill Kramar said. "None of it made any sense. She seemed very confused."

"I just wish we knew what was going on," Aunt Betty said. "After all this time, for her to just show up. It's unbelievable. And now to have little pieces of the puzzle but no big picture . . . it's so upsetting."

"I know you're concerned, Betty," the doctor said. "She's had a rough time and she's hurting. She really needs to be in a hospital for a better examination. Plus there's another problem."

"She keeps asking for Z-Pops," Uncle Bill said sadly. "I heard her."

"What's a Z-Pop?" John asked.

Doc Brimberry hesitated. He looked at John's aunt and uncle. Cousin Lester snorted.

"I can tell you what it is," Cousin Lester said. "It's one of those new illegal drugs. I bet that woman is addicted to it. They say a lot of those Garbage . . . a lot of those people who live out by the dump have problems with drugs."

"A drug?" John asked with surprise.

"Z-Pops is the popular name for a newer synthetic drug called Traginite-Z."

"I've heard of that," John said glumly.

"Traginite-Z is a bad drug indeed," Doc Brimberry said. "It's a compound that contains a drug whose scientific name is Hamartia, a very deadly poison, and another synthetic drug, Douleia. Together, they form

Traginite-Z. Unfortunately, it's extremely addictive to humans and very difficult to get free from."

"So difficult that the ORDER people are putting people like that in their own hospitals," Cousin Lester said. "The government is cracking down on these drug offenders. They're tired of them stealing and causing all kinds of trouble. And I can't say as I blame them."

"But my mom's not like that," John protested. He felt tears coming to her eyes. "She's just sick. Those ORDER people have done something to her. They tricked her somehow."

"We can't be sure what the story is yet," Uncle Bill said solemnly. "All we know is that she needs help, and she needs to go to the hospital, John."

"But what will they do to her there?" John asked. "Will they make her go to some special hospital like Cousin Lester said?"

"I've heard reports of those special hospitals," Uncle Bill said slowly. "But we don't know for sure what your mother needs."

"That's why we must take her in and have her examined more thoroughly," Doc Brimberry said. He patted John on the shoulder. "It's for her own good, John."

"And for our good too," Cousin Lester added. "The sooner she leaves here, the better for everyone. She needs help, and we don't want to get the ORDER people mad at us any more than they already are."

"But doesn't Goliath own the hospital now?" John asked. "I wouldn't trust her with them. They might hurt her."

"We just don't have a choice," Uncle Bill replied. "Doc Brimberry can look in on her, and we trust him. She needs to be in a hospital, John."

"But I don't want her to leave," John said. "She still hasn't told us where my father is. We need to talk to her."

"But she's sleeping," Doc Brimberry said. "She won't be talking to anyone for a while."

"It's for the best, John," Grandfather Kramar said. "The Kings will take care of your mother. You can be sure of that."

"None of you care! None of you know what it's like," John burst out. Then he began to cry. All the confusing emotions poured out of him uncontrollably.

"I won't let you take her. I won't let you take her. She's my mother!"

John wailed as his uncle and aunt led Doc Brimberry back upstairs. Grandfather Kramar held John's sobbing shoulders. But even the old man's touch couldn't soothe him this time. John couldn't bear to watch them take her away. He ran upstairs and then up the small stairs to the attic. He flopped down on the lonely bed and cried. He was still sobbing when the car drove away toward town.

JOHN'S
PLAN
· · · · · · · ·

6

John didn't sleep well that night, nor the
next two nights. His dreams were filled with dark stormy skies with
thunder and lightning. One night in his dream he saw the figure of a
gigantic black snake in the dark storm clouds. The snake, reared back
like a cobra, had red eyes and a white circled X on its chest. The mouth
opened and John saw his mother and father inside, wrapped in chains.
John ran forward, but when he got close to them, the darkness covered
them and the mouth closed. John cried out their names, but the sounds
were swallowed by the darkness. That's when John woke up.

The next few days were agony for John. Aunt Betty and Uncle Bill told him his mother was undergoing tests at the county hospital. But his mother was quarantined, which meant that no one could see her except hospital nurses and doctors. John didn't think that was a good sign. His uncle and grandfather didn't seem very worried that the hospital was owned by Goliath. They had faith in Doc Brimberry's judgment. By Wednesday, John felt he had waited long enough.

"Why can't we see her?" John asked. "She's my mother. What harm would it be to just talk to her?"

"She's still very weak and very sick. She's been unconscious much of the time. Even if you saw her, she couldn't talk to you. She's hardly said a word."

"They think she's crazy, don't they?" John said.

"No one has told us that," Aunt Betty replied.

"There's timing on these things, John," Grandfather Kramar said slowly. He poured cream in his coffee cup. "You have to wait and be patient."

"But I've waited for years already," John said angrily. "It's not fair. Why can't I see my own mother?"

"You can't go in until the doctors give their permission," Aunt Betty said. "And we just don't know when that will be."

"I'm tired of them telling me I can't see my own mother," the boy said to himself. He felt a pain in his neck. "If they won't take me to her, I'll do it myself. After all, I'm her son."

John moped around the house. He finished his schoolwork and then helped clean out the tool shed. As he was cleaning, a plan suddenly occurred to the boy.

John ran out to the workshop. He hopped on his Spirit Flyer bicycle and headed down the driveway. But before he was to the mailbox, the big balloon tires rolled slower and slower until they came to a complete stop.

"Come on, you stupid bike," John said. "I've got to get to town. Why don't you ever work when I need you?"

John stood up on the pedals, but the bike just wobbled and turned sideways. John hopped off as the bike fell. He didn't try to pick it up.

"Stay there, then!" John spat out angrily. "You're no good to me when I really need you."

John felt a twinge of guilt as soon as he said the words, but his anger drowned out his thoughts. He turned and walked toward the road.

The old red bicycle lay in brown weeds next to the driveway.

When John had walked a mile toward town he was already tired, so he stopped to rest. He wondered if he would have time to walk the whole eight miles. Even in his anger he knew that was a long way. A large truck was coming down the road. As it got closer, John recognized the dull gray colors of a truck that belonged to ORDER. John waved his arms as the truck got closer. The big truck slowed down and stopped when it got next to him.

John took a deep breath as he faced the white circled X on the door. The window rolled down. A man in a gray uniform stuck out his head.

"What you need, Sonny?"

"A ride into town."

"That's where I'm headed," the man said. He opened the side door and John climbed up. The truck roared off down the road. The driver didn't say much. When the truck got to the Goliath factory gate, he slowed to a stop and waited for John to get out.

"Thanks, mister," John said as he climbed out. He shut the door. The truck then drove through the gate into the Goliath factory.

John started down Cemetery Road toward town. He felt very much alone and on his own as he jogged the last quarter-mile. Soon he was walking on the old familiar streets of Centerville. He passed by Daniel Bayley's house. He figured Daniel was probably at home, but he didn't stop. He wasn't sure whether Daniel would help him or not.

John knew right where he wanted to go. He walked through the town square, past the courthouse, and turned east. Soon he was walking down a street filled with houses. He turned up a walk and knocked on a door.

He waited.

"Come on, be home," John muttered impatiently.

The door opened. Roger Darrow stood there in his gray Commando uniform. He seemed surprised to see John.

"What are you doing here?" Roger asked.

"I need your help," John replied.

Roger looked confused. For years, he and John had been close friends. But all that had changed since John had gotten a Spirit Flyer bicycle and Goliath Industries had come to town. "What do you want?" Roger asked. At least he didn't sound too unfriendly, John thought.

"Your mom still works at the county hospital, right?" John asked.

"Yeah, sure," Roger replied.

"I need to get in there to see someone," John explained. "I was hoping you and Rick could take me over there in Rick's car."

"You want to go see your mother, don't you?" Roger said.

"How did you know?" John asked.

"I heard she came back. My mom told me. Everyone is real surprised since we all thought she was dead."

"Well, she's not dead," John said firmly. "And I think she knows where my father is, but I can't find out because they won't let any of us talk to her."

"I heard she was real sick," Roger said. "They've got her in one of those special quarantined rooms."

"I've got to see her," John said. "And you can help me if you want to. Can't you ask Rick to take me over there? I won't have to be with her long. And you know your way around the hospital, don't you?"

"Well, yeah, I guess so," Roger said. He frowned as he was thinking. "Rick isn't here. Let me go make some telephone calls."

Roger closed the door, and John sat down on the front step to wait. About ten minutes later, Rick Darrow, Roger's seventeen-year-old brother, drove up in a small blue pickup. The front door opened and Roger get out.

"Let's go," he said matter-of-factly. "We can get you to the hospital, but I can't guarantee you'll get inside."

"Thanks, Roger," John said. He held out his hand. Roger shook it, though he seemed uneasy.

The ride to Kirksville took twenty minutes. The sky was getting dark as they pulled up to County General Hospital. In the lower right-hand corner of the hospital's sign were a circled white X and the words, *A Goliath Company.*

"We better go in a side door," Roger said.

"I'm going to the music store," Rick Darrow said. "I'll be back for you guys in an hour. Be ready or I'm leaving you. I've got homework to do tonight."

John and Roger nodded. They got out and walked up the sidewalk as the little blue pickup pulled away. Two ambulances were parked in the driveway along the sidewalk, as well as two dark gray ORDER emergency vehicles.

Roger led John around the back of the hospital to a solid metal door. He opened it, and they both went inside. The first thing John noticed was the smell. The hospital had a chemical, antiseptic odor.

"This is the back stairs," Roger said. "Your mom is on the top floor."

"How do you know?" John asked.

Roger hesitated, looking confused.

"Well, ah . . . I think I heard my mom mention it," Roger said finally. "I mean, the quarantine area is on that floor, so she must be up there. But maybe I should make sure. I'll go check at the front desk. You wait here."

Roger walked down the hall toward the lobby. At the front desk, he talked to the receptionist and then walked over to the security guard. The guard wore a gray ORDER uniform like Roger's.

"Peace and safety," the guard said, crossing his arm over his chest. "I was told you were coming. Where's your friend?"

"He's in the back stairway," Roger said. "I was going to take him upstairs to the fourth floor."

"We'll be ready," the guard said. "We appreciate your loyalty. Once he tries to enter, we'll get him. Your payment will show up on your Number Card account by tomorrow."

"They won't hurt him, will they?" Roger asked.

"Not at all," the guard said. "But he will be charged with trespassing, and it will become part of his record. These Rank Blank kids need to be taught who's the boss."

"I better get back," Roger said. He walked away from the lobby, back down the hallway toward the stairs. He opened the door.

"It's just like I thought," Roger said. "She's in room 417 . . ."

Roger looked around. The hallway was empty. John wasn't in sight. The boy in the gray uniform quickly opened the outside door. But John was nowhere to be seen. Roger stepped back inside. Then he looked up the stairs. He began running toward the fourth floor.

John had been too impatient to wait for Roger. He had started climbing the stairs a minute after Roger had left. He had run up the stairs two at a time. He was out of breath by the time he got to the top floor. A big red number 4 was painted on the door that led inside. John took a few gulps of air and opened the door slowly. The hallway was empty. The hospital smell was even stronger. Off to the right were two big swinging doors. John's heart pounded when he saw the words, "Quarantine Section. Do Not Enter Except By Permission. No Exceptions."

John walked slowly toward the doors. He peeped around the corner. A woman pushing a cart was moving down the hall toward him. John pulled his head back quickly. She stopped in front of the quarantine section. She put on rubber gloves and a mask over her face. She pushed a large red button on the wall next to the door frame. Immediately the two doors swung open. She pushed the car through and the doors closed behind her. John waited.

No one was in the hallway. He walked over to the doors. He peeked through the glass. Inside was another set of glass doors. Beyond them he could see a short hallway with six closed doors. The woman with the cart was nowhere in sight.

"Help me, please," John said. He pushed the red button on the wall and waited. The two doors swung open. John stepped inside the little room. The doors shut behind him. He pushed on the one of the glass doors and it opened. On the wall next to one door he saw the name *Kramar*. He walked over and peeked through the glass rectangle on the door. He saw a bed and a person lying on the bed. John opened the door and stepped inside, trying to be as quiet as possible.

Just as the door closed, he saw another door out in the hallway open. The woman pushing the cart was coming right toward his mother's room. John felt a surge of fear as he stepped back. He felt a doorknob press into his back. He whirled around and turned the knob. The door opened into a small closet. John quickly stepped into the closet. A few seconds later, he heard the room door open and the sound of the rolling cart.

"I have your medicine for you, Ms. Kramar," a woman said loudly. John heard the cart stop rolling. He let out his breath, which he realized he had been holding for several seconds. Just as he took a big gulp of air, he heard the room door open again. Heavy steps walked past the closet.

"We had a report that an unauthorized person, a boy, was coming up to this room," a man's voice said. John supposed it belonged to a security guard. Then he wondered what had happened to Roger. It didn't cross his mind that his old friend had tried to double-cross him. "No one's in here," the woman's voice replied. "I just got up here and haven't seen anyone. He must not have gotten here yet."

"OK, but just to make sure, we'll be using the key lock on this wing until we find him," the man's voice said. "I'll be waiting outside to let you out. Just be sure to let security know if you see any stray boys wandering around."

"I'll just be a minute more," the woman said. The heavy steps walked back across the room. The door opened and shut. Then John heard the cart rolling across the floor. The door opened again and the cart rolled out. After the door shut, John heard a clicking noise. He waited and waited in the dark closet for what seemed like hours but really was just a few minutes.

"It's now or never," John said softly to himself. He opened the door slowly. He peeked out. Seeing no one, he pushed the door open further. He stepped into the room. He didn't see anyone out in the hall outside the room. He walked quickly back toward the bed.

His mother was sitting up. She looked thin and pale, almost as white as the white sheets. She stared at John for a long time.

"Mother!" John said. He ran to the bed. He bent down and laid his head on her lap. Tears filled the boy's eyes. "Mother, I've come to help you. Please let me help you."

COUNTY
GENERAL
HOSPITAL
· · · · · · · ·
7

John lifted his face from his mother's lap. She stared at him. Her eyes seemed weary and tired. Her hands trembled as he took them into his own.

"What happened, Mother?" John asked. "Where have you been? Why didn't you come home sooner? Where's Dad? Is he alive? Did he survive the storm? Did you see a big snake in the storm?"

His mother's eyes opened wider. Fear flashed across her face.

"Don't make me go back," she said. "They thought I was dead, but I got away. I got away from them. They wanted to keep me locked up in that casket, but I got away. Joe said not to leave, but I had to. I had to leave."

"Leave where?" John asked. He held his mother's hands. She looked out into the room at nothing as she talked.

"They took us in that storm. It was all a lie and a trick," his mother said. "They took us away. We had to go or they would have killed us. We had to go. They would have gotten our baby."

"But I am safe," John said. "I'm your son."

Mary looked at John with wild eyes. She squinted, then cocked her head.

"I'm your son, John Kramar," John said. He smiled.

"Everything died in the storm," she said. "Nothing was left for us. So we joined them. We had to do it. They gave us work. We had plenty of work, but my back hurt all the time."

"What happened in the storm?" John asked gently. "Did you see a big snake? A snake as big as a tornado?"

"He was big," Mary said, nodding her head. "The rain kept falling and falling. I thought it would never stop. Grinsby wanted to make a deal. He had offered us a lot of money for our Spirit Flyers. Business was bad. Joe was scared it wouldn't work out. He wanted to listen to Grinsby's deal."

"I remember a man named Grinsby," John said. "He came around here last year."

"We took off one night in the rain," his mother said. "We didn't take John with us. We met Grinsby. He had an old black truck. We got in the truck and it smelled bad. Then the tornado got our car. He told us we all would die. Joe said we had to do what he said."

The woman's eyes were wide with fear. She seemed to be watching the whole scene happen over again.

"Did you try to escape?" John asked.

"Grinsby said we'd made a deal," Mary Kramar said in a cracking voice. "We were too afraid to run. He had all that money. Joe got wrapped in that chain. I cried, I was so scared. And then the chains were all around me. I was so afraid and ashamed. I knew we shouldn't have been there in the first place. He tricked us good."

"But what happened?" John asked. He shook his mother's hands. "What happened next? Why were you gone so long?"

"They lied," his mother said as she began to cry. "They lied and told me I would feel better. I don't feel better. I want a Z-Pop. Can't I have one? I need some right now."

"What happened to Dad? Is he alive? Did Grinsby kill him?"

"He's not dead," she grunted. "He spent all the money and now he has to live with the pigs. He's calling the hogs every day—he looks like a pig himself, wallowing in the mud."

"Why do you say that? Where is he? Is he alive?"

"He's in that scary house now, calling the hogs."

"What do you mean?" John insisted. "Where is he?"

"He's at the Gardens," his mother murmured.

"What gardens?

"Goliath Gardens," she said in a monotone. "That's where we worked for them. But I ran away. I couldn't take it no more, being in that dark house, lying in that casket. I had to get away. I don't care if I die. I don't care anymore about anything. I'm so ashamed and afraid . . . I'm so ashamed . . . I just wanted to come home to die."

Tears came slowly out of his mother's eyes. She didn't make a sound as she stared off into the room, looking back into some secret hidden shame that she could see so well. But all John saw was his mother's tears. He took a tissue and wiped her eyes.

"Don't cry, Mother," John said. "You don't have to cry. You don't have to die. You're home now. We'll help you, no matter what happens . . ."

His mother shook her head back and forth, as if to refuse his offer of mercy, her lips quivering. She lifted her right arm.

"I need a Z-Pop. I want some bad. Can't you get one?" she said. For the first time John noticed bruises on the inside of her arm and wondered why they were there. "I'd feel better if I had a Z-Pop."

John reached to get another tissue. Just as he was dabbing the tears off his mother's cheeks, the door suddenly opened. John whirled around to see two security guards in gray uniforms scowling at him. Before he could move they had grabbed him by the arms.

"We found him!" one man said. He pulled John toward the door.

"Let me talk to my mother!" John cried out. But he was no match for the two men. Without being able to look back, he was dragged out of the room. "Let me go!" John said. He kicked one the security guards on the shin, and the man let go. But the other held tight. John struggled and yelled all the way to the elevator.

The elevator hummed as it dropped. By the time the doors opened, John gave up struggling. He knew it was useless. The two men led him out into the hall. John saw Roger standing next to a desk with other security guards. Roger didn't say anything as they led John past him. They led down John another hall and stopped in front of a small room.

"You'll stay in here until the police and your parents come to get you," the guard said. "You won't cause any more trouble if you know what's good for you."

They put him inside and closed the door. The lock clicked behind him. The room had two chairs and no windows. John sat down and waited. Feelings of fear and anger and dread settled on him as the time passed.

He kept running over in his mind what his mother had said. But not much of it made sense. They had seen Grinsby and made some sort of deal, but the rest was too confusing. He still didn't understand why they hadn't come home if they had been alive. And it seemed as if his mother was sure his father was alive, living at the Goliath Gardens amusement park.

After a while, two security guards returned with another man in a police uniform. The man in the police uniform held an aluminum clipboard. He looked at John and then read a sheet on the clipboard.

"John, I'm Sergeant Anderson," the policeman said. "I understand you

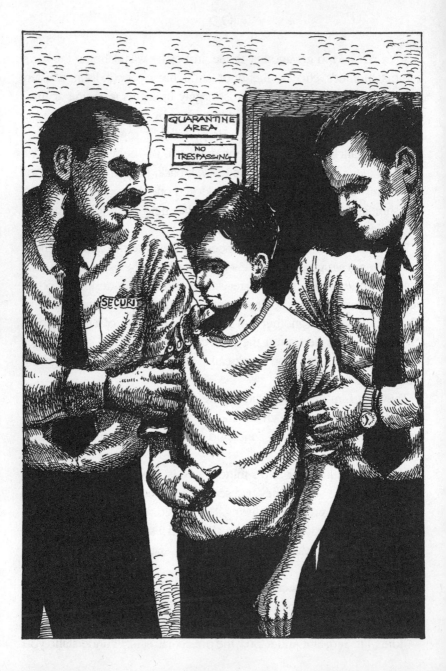

don't have a number card. Is that correct?"

"I don't have a card," John said.

"You're in big trouble, son," the policeman said. "I'm told you have been trespassing here and disturbing sick patients, not to mention assaulting one of our guards."

"I was talking to my mother," John said glumly. "Is that a crime?"

"It is the way you did it, yes, indeed," the policeman said. "There are all sorts of charges against you. We can go right down to the station tonight. Would you like that?"

"No," John said quietly.

"I didn't think so," Sergeant Anderson said. "The hospital doesn't want trouble and neither do we. We're willing to make a deal on this matter, and your parents don't even have to find out."

"A deal?" John asked.

"That's right," Sergeant Anderson replied. "The hospital and the sheriff's office will agree to drop all charges if you sign a simple statement saying you will not trespass illegally on the hospital grounds."

"OK," John said slowly. He didn't see how he could get out of it.

"You must also do your civic duty and get a current number card."

"Why do I have to do that?" John demanded. "What's that have to do with anything?"

"It has everything to do with everything, boy," Sergeant Anderson said with a frown. "Where have you been for the last six months? We can't process your statement unless you have a current functioning number card, and there's no deal if we can't have your signed statement in complete form. The hospital has a CardMaker here on the premises in the admissions room. You will accompany these two guards, get your card, and sign the statement. Unless you want to go with us to the jail and have us notify your legal guardians, your aunt and uncle."

John knew he would be in big trouble if Uncle Bill found out that he had defied his order and tried to come to the hospital alone. At the same time he didn't want the card. He felt trapped.

"I'll get my card," John said, not wanting to face his uncle or his grandfather. "At least I can get library books with it," he thought. "Maybe it won't be so bad."

The two guards walked side by side with John down long hallways. Sergeant Anderson followed. At the end of one hallway, they went into a small room. A number card machine was in the center of the room.

The machine was like a large black box. John stuck his face up to a hole in the side of the box. A flash blinded his eyes. In a few seconds, a small black card about the size of a credit card dropped out of a slot. Sergeant Anderson took the card and began writing on his clipboard. Ten minutes later he was done. They escorted John to the front doors of the hospital and watched him go outside. The security guards smiled.

"That's one scared Rank Blank kid," one guard said.

"Well, they have to be taught a lesson," Sergeant Anderson said grimly. "The main thing headquarters wanted on him was to get him to compromise. If they compromise once, they'll do it again. That's how you break these rebellious ones."

The security guards nodded and laughed. They watched John carefully.

Outside, John looked down at the shiny black card and felt guilty. Part of him knew he shouldn't have gotten the card, but the other part didn't want to get into trouble with his uncle or grandfather.

"I *had* to get the card," John said to himself. He looked around. "I wonder what happened to Rick and Roger. He promised he'd wait."

Off in the distance, the clouds rumbled. The night was coming. "What if I have to call Uncle Bill to come get me? He'll find out about what happened."

John looked up and down the street. He turned and looked back inside the hospital. The two guards were by the reception desk, looking out at him. John turned away.

He felt in his pockets for money. Hearing a familiar horn, he looked up. Coming up the street were two people on bicycles. As they got closer, John recognized Susan and Daniel Bayley. John waved. They waved back and rode up.

"We thought you were in trouble," Susan said excitedly. "Our Spirit Flyers brought us here. I was at the house when the horn on my bike sounded, and I thought of you right away. When I got on the Spirit Flyer, it took off. Daniel saw you in the mirror of his bike just before it started going on its own. We met in the sky just beyond the cemetery in Centerville. Then our Spirit Flyers brought us here. Are you all right? You're not hurt, are you?"

"No, I'm fine," John said quickly.

"But why are you at the hospital if you aren't hurt?" Daniel asked.

"I came to see my mother," John said.

"But I thought she wasn't allowed to see anyone," Susan asked. "Did they change their mind?"

"Well, sort of," John said slowly. "I just talked to her for a little while. But I'm glad you're here. We better leave before Uncle Bill misses us."

"But how did you get here?" Susan asked. She looked concerned.

"Roger Darrow's brother, Rick, brought me," John said. "We better get going. I'll ride on the back of Daniel's bike."

"Wait a minute," Susan said. She frowned as she looked at John. "Why would Roger Darrow's brother bring you here? They haven't been friendly with you in a long time. Something doesn't add up here."

"I guess they wanted to be nice," John said. "Why are you acting so suspicious?"

"I'm not being suspicious," Susan replied. "But you seem jumpy or upset. What really happened, John?"

"Nothing," John insisted as he climbed on the back of Daniel's old red bicycle. "I wanted to see my mother, and I did. Now it's time to go home."

"But the horn on my bike sounded," Susan said. "It was the warning sound, like someone's in trouble."

"I got the same impression too," Daniel said. "I saw you in a room with some guards or something and one of those number card machines. I thought you were being forced to get a number card or something like that."

"Don't be silly," John said nervously. "Let's get home before we get in trouble. Roger's brother just left me here, and the Spirit Flyers must have known I needed a ride home."

"I still don't get it," Susan said, shaking her head. "Are you telling us everything?" She stared at John.

He tried to smile and shrugged his shoulders. The number card in his front pants pocket bit into his leg like the edge of a blade. "I told you what happened," he said. "Let's get home before the storm comes and we get soaked."

Susan sighed. Daniel began to pedal down the street. Soon both bikes were zooming up into the darkening sky. In the distance, lightning flashed and was followed by the sound of rumbling thunder.

THE NUMBER CARD HAS AN IDEA
········

They got home before the rain hit, but just barely. Steaming bowls of food waited on the blue-and-white tablecloth and the family had just sat down at the dinner table, about to start eating, when John and Susan came into the dining room. Cousin Lester frowned when he saw them.

"Where have you two been?" Uncle Bill asked.

"We were out," John said, trying to avoid the discussion.

"John went to see his mother in the hospital!" Susan blurted out.

"You did?" Aunt Betty asked.

"I thought no one was allowed to see her," Cousin Lester said as he piled mashed potatoes on his plate. Everyone paused. Uncle Lester ate twice as much as anyone else, yet he was always thin. He reached for the meat and gravy and began a second pile next to the potatoes. "I thought she was in quarantine. Hospitals don't usually let you see people in quarantine."

"I saw her," John said softly. He looked down at his plate, quickly dipping out spoonfuls. "They didn't let me see her for long, but I did get to see her."

"Even in quarantine?" his aunt asked. "Maybe it's because you're her son that they let you in."

Uncle Bill stared at John. He frowned as if wanting to ask a question.

"But that's not the only part," Susan said excitedly. "His mom acted like she knew where John's dad was."

"Really?" Grandfather Kramar asked. "When I asked her about Joe, she didn't seem to understand me."

"She said something about him calling the hogs, like he's a farmer or something," John said quickly. "Then she said something about being at Goliath Gardens."

"Goliath Gardens?" Uncle Bill asked. "That's the fancy amusement park down near the capital, isn't it?"

"It's in the town of Avown, which is near the capital," Aunt Betty said. "It used to be called WonderRama World. We took the kids there the year before Goliath bought it. They've really turned it into a tourist spot since then."

"I've always wanted to go back there," John said, "ever since I heard about the changes. I think we should go for sure, now that we know Dad may be there. We've got to go."

"That place is as expensive as they come," Cousin Lester said. "We went there, but I wouldn't pay twice for the experience. It's just a bunch of con men trying to get your hard-earned money to spend on some foolishness and games."

"But my father may be there," John said. "We've got to go find out."

The table was quiet for a moment. Cousin Lester and Lester, Jr., were busy chewing. John looked back and forth between his uncle and his grandfather.

"I think we should check into the possibility," Grandfather Kramar said. "But I think Bill and I should talk to your mother first. If she confirms that Goliath Gardens is where she thinks Joe is, then we can go down there and check it out."

"And I'll go with you, right?" John asked.

"I think your granddad and I ought to go alone first, to see what the situation is," Uncle Bill said.

"I think your uncle's right, John," Grandfather Kramar said. "If your dad isn't there, it will be a long trip and a disappointment. And if he is there, then there must be some reason why he hasn't shown his face around here for so many years. I think we ought to check it out first and not rush into anything."

"But what if he's really alive?" John demanded. His voice was rising. "I've got to go see him, don't you see? He's my father!"

"And he's my son, and Bill's brother," Grandfather Kramar said. "We're all anxious to see him, if he's there. But there's a timing to things, John, the King's timing. You don't put on your shoes, then your socks, remember? How you get something done is just as important as what you're trying to do in the first place. In the kingdom, you can't take shortcuts. You have to be patient."

"I don't see why I couldn't go with you," John protested.

"We don't know that we're going anywhere yet," Uncle Bill said. "Your mother is still very sick. She might have been confused when you talked to her."

"She still didn't look very good," John said softly. "And she was asking for those Z-Pop things."

"I knew it," Cousin Lester said, still chewing. "That woman is messed up on some awful drug, mark my words. And who knows if she's got something contagious. I can't believe they let a boy go in and see a quarantined woman."

"None of you understand anything!" John said, feeling his voice rise in frustration. "We've got to go find my dad. He might need us. He could be a prisoner if he's working for Goliath. My mom said they were tricked."

"Tricked? How were they tricked?" Grandfather Kramar asked. He looked carefully at the boy.

"I'm not sure exactly," John said. "She said that Grinsby offered them a lot of money a long time ago."

"You mean the man who was mixed up in those bicycle thefts last June?" Uncle Bill asked.

"It sounded like the same guy," John said. "She didn't really describe him. Anyway, she said that he offered them a lot of money, and they were tricked somehow. It all happened around the time of those storms a long time ago when their car was wrecked. If she's alive, he must be alive too."

"I don't know what to make of it for sure," Grandfather Kramar said. "But we need to talk to your mother first."

"I agree," Uncle Bill said. "We don't want to waste a lot of time and money going on some wild goose chase."

"The whole thing sounds like a crazy tale and foolishness if you ask me," Cousin Lester said. He spooned up the very last dribbles of gravy. "That woman is a very sick person. Why you would trust her opinion on anything is beyond me."

"But she's the only one who knows!" John said loudly. He wanted to say something else to Cousin Lester but stopped.

"We'll go to the hospital again and see if we can talk to your mother," Uncle Bill said. "She's the only one who can shed light on this situation."

John slept uneasily in the attic that night. Outside, the wind howled as the rain fell. In his dreams, a storm was raging just as fiercely. John was running in the empty Centerville streets at night with a black, six-foot number card chasing him. He heard his father calling his name over and over, but as John ran through the streets, he couldn't seem to get away from the number card or get any closer to his father's voice. A big crack of lightning struck right by him as he was running and he woke up. Outside the tiny attic window, lightning lit up the sky, followed by a tremendous crack of thunder. For a long time John looked out at the rainy night sky. All he could think about was finding his father.

The next day, Grandfather Kramar and Uncle Bill rode away around ten in the morning. They were going to run some errands, but the main reason for the trip was to go to the hospital. John rushed through his schoolwork. His mind was really not on the work anyway, and his Aunt Betty could see that.

When Uncle Bill's pickup truck pulled into the driveway late in the afternoon, John jumped up from his desk and ran outside. Uncle Bill and Grandfather Kramar were both carrying some packages.

"Did you talk to my mom?" John blurted out. "What did she say? Did she tell you about my father?"

"We need help with these packages," Uncle Bill told John. "There's more in the back of the truck."

John ran to the side of the truck and got as many packages as he could hold. He scurried after his uncle and grandfather, trying not to drop anything.

Inside, the two men set the packages on the table in the kitchen. John hurriedly dumped his packages next to theirs.

"Did you see her?" he asked, almost out of breath. "What did she say?"

"We saw her," Uncle Bill said seriously. He didn't seem as excited as John thought he would be.

"What did she say?" John asked. "Did she say anything about my dad?"

"John, we saw your mother through a window," Grandfather Kramar said slowly. "But she wasn't doing well. She's a very sick woman, very sick."

"What do you mean?" John asked.

"We didn't get to talk to her," Uncle Bill said. "Apparently last night she went unconscious, and they weren't able to wake her. They think she may be in a coma of some kind, according to the doctor."

"She isn't dead, is she?"

"No, she isn't dead, but she is very sick and the doctors aren't sure what to do," Grandfather Kramar said. "She's breathing fine. But she's just very sick, that's all. They don't understand what's happened for sure."

"Why can't they just wake her up?" John asked. His voice cracked. He was beginning to feel afraid. He had never thought his mother was seriously ill till now.

"It's not that simple," Uncle Bill said. "According to the doctor, sometime these kinds of episodes last a few hours or sometimes they last for days, or even longer."

"How long?" John asked. Both his uncle and grandfather looked at the floor.

"We just don't know what to think, John," his grandfather said. "We're all very sorry. The doctor told us they were doing everything they could to help her."

"You mean she might die?" John asked.

"We don't know what to expect," Grandfather Kramar said softly. "But if things take a turn for the worse, that's a possibility."

"But she can't die," John cried out. "Not again. We just got her back!"

"John, we all feel very bad about this situation," Uncle Bill said. "Our hopes were just as high as yours when your mother first arrived. But we have to face reality. She's still very sick."

"Then we've got to go get my father," John said. "I bet he could help. I know he could. I think we should leave right now. Let's just get in the truck and go find him."

"John, we don't know where your father is for sure, or if he's really alive," Grandfather Kramar said. "Whatever your mother told you, she told you when she was very sick. She could have been talking about things that happened years ago. There are still too many missing pieces to this puzzle."

"But those are the only pieces we've got left!" John cried out.

"We plan to look into it," Uncle Bill said. "We tried calling down there, but no one would talk to us without number card identification. Your grandfather and I may even go down there at the end of the week. But we've got other responsibilities here. Number Day will soon be on us, and we have to be prepared for the changes we'll be facing. We've been talking to some of the people who used to live at the dump, and they need a place to stay. Some may be moving to the farm, and we will need to help them."

"But we've got to go find my dad now!" John insisted. "Don't you understand? He may be able to help her."

"Like I told you before," his grandfather said, "there's a timing to things, John. We have to wait on the King's timing. I want to find your dad, but I don't feel peaceful about it yet, and I'm not sure why. But I think we'll go soon."

"I've waited long enough!" John cried out. "I don't think you really care. Nobody cares anymore but me."

John ran out of the room. He hit the front door and ran down the steps. He kept running and running and running. When he finally stopped, he realized he was out in the cornfield, half a mile away from the house, near a big pond. John slowly walked toward the pond, lost in his thoughts.

"None of them care," John muttered to himself. He kicked the ground. Nothing seemed to make sense. He didn't see how his uncle and grandfather could be so unconcerned. He picked up a rock and threw it into the pond. He threw another and another as he stood there.

"I've got to do something," he said to himself. "Dad would come help if he knew Mom was sick. I know he's alive. I know he'd help. I've got to figure out a way."

John stood by the pond for over an hour, throwing rocks and thinking.

He kept seeing his mother's pale face. He tried to imagine his father's face. He had pictures of his father, of course, but they were from years ago. But he had pictures of his mother and he hadn't recognized her.

"If only Grandfather Kramar would help me," John said softly. He walked home, feeling hopeful that he could convince his uncle and grandfather to go look for his father.

But John was disappointed. Both his uncle and grandfather said they needed to wait at least a few days. They were busy with farm work. They also went to several meetings of the Spirit Flyer clubs. Everyone was worried about Number Day and the coming changes. John had stopped going to the meetings because the people always seemed to argue about so many things. No one could agree what to do. They argued about number cards and ORDER. They argued about whether or not to help the people at the dump. They even argued about whether or not to ride their Spirit Flyers. His grandfather and uncle didn't seem to get discouraged about all the disagreements in the meetings, but John hated to hear them argue.

On Friday night, John lay on his bed in the attic, looking up at the ceiling. In his hand he held the black plastic number card with his face on it. When he stuck his thumb on the print square, the card came to life: *John Kramar*—Rank Blank; Negative number: 17, Sector 55, Cell 283.

John looked at the card in his hand. The shadowy image of his face stared back at him. He still felt guilty for having the card. He hadn't told anyone and didn't intend to tell.

"I had to do it," John said softly to himself. "I had to see her. Besides, at least I can get library books with this card. Maybe number cards aren't so bad. Most everyone has them. And when Number Day comes, what will we do if we don't have them? We won't be able to buy anything without them." The face on John's card almost seemed to glow. John blinked. He looked at the card more closely. The eyes almost seemed to turn red. John shook his head and rubbed his own eyes.

He looked at the card again.

"You did the right thing. Everyone knows it," the face on the card suddenly spoke. John sat up, holding the card away from his body. The face on the card laughed. "Why don't you wise up, you idiot? Everyone has a number card. It's the only game in town, remember? Why fight progress? You can't beat them, so why not join them?"

"That's right," John said, shaking his head sadly. "Why fight them? They'll win in the end. I even heard Grandfather Kramar saying something like that one night, that they might convince everyone to their way of thinking."

"That's right," the face on the card said. "You have other things to think about, like finding your dad. You need to go get him and bring him home, don't you? Your uncle and grandfather don't care. You need to take action and do it fast!"

"That's right," John said. "I do need to go get him. But how?"

"Use your money, you idiot," the face said. "Take your savings. It won't be any good after Number Day. You can be down at Goliath Gardens when it opens and find your father right away. You'll even be a hero when you bring him back home. You'll save your mother too. You'd like to be a hero again, wouldn't you?"

"I could save them all," John said to himself. "I'll just go do it. I don't need their help. I don't need anyone's help."

"You need my help," the shadowy face on the card said. "Don't forget what counts."

"That's right," John said. "I probably will need the number card, especially if I want to get into Goliath Gardens."

John hopped out of bed. He opened the bottom desk drawer and got out a metal box with a small padlock on it. He shook it. All his savings were inside.

"Tomorrow is Saturday, and I'll do it," John said to himself. He shook the box full of money again. "Tomorrow I'll fix everything, they'll see. Tomorrow I'll go find my father . . ."

INSIDE GOLIATH GARDENS

· · · · · · · ·

9

John woke up early the next morning. He had breakfast before the others and ran outside to the workshop. A wad of money filled his right front pocket—all his savings. John reached down to touch it, to make sure it was still there. When he got inside the workshop, he closed the doors behind him. He walked over quickly to his red Spirit Flyer bicycle.

John smiled. The chain was greased and the tires were pumped up and ready to go. As he remembered all the good times he had had on the old bicycle, he felt a sudden pain in the back of his neck. John reached up to rub the hurting place. Then he remembered the number card. He had made sure to bring it along for insurance. He pulled it out of his back pocket.

He stared at his shadowy image in the card. The face almost seemed to smile.

"I won't use the card unless I absolutely have to," John said softly.

"You need me," the face on the card seemed to say. John's eyes opened wider when he realized the lips on his picture actually seemed to move.

"I must be a little anxious," John said to himself.

"Of course you are," the face said. "You're on an important mission. You're going to find your dad and save him and your mom and finally be happy after all these years of belonging to no one."

"That's not really true," John said to himself. "I've been happy with Uncle Bill and Aunt Betty. They've taken good care of me."

"But you know it's not the same," the face replied. "You were an obligation, an added burden on them. You aren't their *real* son."

"Well, I'm not their biological son," John said. "But they adopted me and they treat me like a son."

"Adopted. What's that? You were just an obligation, not the real thing," the face said. "You're just afraid to admit it."

"I am not," John said.

"You're afraid, all right," the face said. "Just like you're afraid to admit your own real parents abandoned you because they didn't want you."

"That's not true," John said out loud. He was surprised to hear his voice protesting in the early morning silence of the workshop. "This is silly, talking to myself."

He took a step toward the Spirit Flyer, but the voice on the card spoke again.

"You don't think that bike is going to help you, do you?" the face asked, sounding very disgusted.

"Spirit Flyers always help," John said. "They're a gift from the kings."

"Sure they are," the face said. "Remember when you tried to go see your mom the other day? It wouldn't even roll out of the driveway. Do you think it's going to be any different for your dad? That bike's not going anywhere. You can bet on it."

John stopped. The voice seemed to be making sense. He remembered how angry he was when the old bicycle wouldn't work when he had set out to see his mother.

"It didn't work then, did it?" John said to himself.

"Of course not, and you're wasting your time even trying today," the voice replied. "You'd better get into town and take the bus. That's the best way to get there. And you'd better hurry before the others find out you're gone or they'll stop you. They don't want you to find your father, do they? They don't care at all."

"Well, I care," John said. So without seeing what would happen if he got on the old red bike, he walked out of the workshop. He slammed the big door behind him and looked toward the house. He didn't see anyone outside or through the windows.

"Run for it, before they stop you," the voice on the card said, sounding more and more like himself. So John ran. He ran down the driveway and onto Glory Road. He didn't stop running until the house was completely out of sight.

John had been walking toward Centerville for twenty minutes when a farmer in an old pickup truck came by. John stuck out his thumb. Mr. Mulberry knew John and gave him a ride into town.

Mr. Mulberry parked on the south side of the town square. John got a drink at the water fountain by the old gazebo and then walked quickly down South Main Street toward the bus depot.

The round-trip ticket to the capital cost more than John had imagined. It took more than half his money. But there was nothing else to do but pay it.

After the cashier had counted his money, she asked for his number card. John handed it to her.

"Avown?" she asked."You must be going to Goliath Gardens. Our whole family went last Saturday, which was opening day. We had a great time. It's expensive though."

"That's what I hear," John replied, hoping she'd just give him the ticket. She put the number card in a slot and hit some buttons. A few seconds later, the printed ticket was ready. She gave John the ticket and his number card.

"The bus leaves in five minutes," she said. "You better get on now."

John walked quickly to the bus. As he passed a telephone, he thought about calling home to let them know where he was going.

"Call home? What for?" the face on the number card demanded. "If they really loved you, they'd be taking you down themselves. You wouldn't have had to spend so much money on a bus ticket. If you call, they'll try to stop you."

"You're right," John said. "Uncle Bill wouldn't let me go. But I've got to go."

John found the bus, gave the driver the ticket and got on. In a few minutes, the bus rolled onto Main Street and headed south. When the bus pulled onto the state highway from Main, they were out of the Centerville city limits. John looked back at the water tower in town, and then faced forward, wondering if he would find his father.

The bus ride seemed to take forever to the boy. He read magazines and a paperback book someone had left in another seat. A few hours past lunch, the bus arrived in the state capital. John boarded another bus. Thirty minutes later he got off in front of Goliath Gardens.

John stared up at a huge sign which said: "Goliath Gardens—Featuring the Gardens of Delight." In the distance, behind tall green walls of vegetation and cement, rides were sticking up into the sky. He saw Ferris wheels, parachute drops, a water slide, a falling, spinning spaceship machine that was only for children or adults with a strong stomach. John wasn't familiar with several of the rides.

But the one ride towering above all the rest was the Goliath Three, a monster of a roller coaster, advertised as one of the largest roller

coasters in the world. In tall towers like mountains, the Goliath Three stood in the middle of Goliath Gardens, the main attraction. Every kid boasted about riding the Goliath and not being scared. John had heard many children talk about it. In the distance, John could see a car rolling slowly to the top of the first mountain in the roller coaster. Even from far away he could hear the screams as the car zoomed down the hill.

Waiting in line for his ticket, he was surprised how many families were going inside. The weather seemed extra sunny and warm for April.

The person selling the tickets was dressed like a giant wolf. The fake teeth looked very real and sharp.

"You paying with cash?" the big wolf asked. "I haven't seen any cash all day. Everyone's using the number cards now. I'll be glad when we all use them. Only one more week left until Number Day. The cards are quicker, and you don't have to waste time giving out change."

"There's not much change to give," John said sadly, as he received back a single bill and some coins.

"I need your number card," the wolf said. John gave him the black plastic card. The man put it in a small black box. He looked surprised.

"Rank Blank, eh?" the wolf asked. "And you come all the way from Centerville? Where's your family, kid?"

"They'll be by later," John said quickly. As soon as he said it, he knew he was lying, but he was afraid they wouldn't let him in.

"You say they'll be by later?"

"That's right," John said.

The man didn't say anything. The black box whirred and a ticket came out of a slot. The man gave it to John.

"Have fun in Goliath Gardens, kid," the man with a wolf mask said. John took the ticket and went through the turnstile. As soon as he had walked away, the man inside the booth picked up a blue telephone. He waited. "This is Booth 3. That reported runaway kid just went through my booth. He paid with cash . . . Yeah, it was the kid from Centerville.

. . . OK, it's your turn now."

The man with the wolf mask hung up the phone and laughed.

John wandered around Goliath Gardens. He was amazed by all the rides and booths and restaurants and stores. Everywhere he went, he saw smiling faces.

Now that he was there, he wasn't sure where to begin. Not only that, he was hungry, and he hardly had enough money for a hot dog and a soda.

"Are you John Kramar?" a voice said behind him.

John turned around. A short stocky man wearing a gray ORDER uniform stood in front of John.

"Are you John Kramar?" the man asked again. He didn't look very friendly.

"Yes," John said slowly. "Is something wrong?"

"The management wants to talk to you," the man said stiffly. "We heard reports about a runaway boy."

John's heart leaped to his throat. As the man stepped forward, John jumped back.

"Hey, come here!" the man said.

But John didn't wait around. He turned and ran through the line of people waiting for the roller coaster. He darted around a corner of a building and ran back underneath the roller coaster, hiding behind a tall pillar. The guard came running around the building. He didn't slow down but kept running down the midway. John walked underneath the tall roller coaster. After a while, his heart stopped beating so hard.

"Now I can't ask about my father," John moaned. "If I ask about Joe Kramar, they'll get suspicious. How did they find out about me?"

John wandered past rides and booths. One part of Goliath Gardens had farm animals and other animals one might find at a zoo. John looked around, seeing if there was anyone who looked like the old photograph he had of his father. He sort of knew what to look for since his father resembled Uncle Bill. But the picture was years old. John wondered if he would recognize his father even if he saw him.

There was no one in the animal exhibit. John asked a woman tending some baby pigs if she knew Joe Kramar, but the woman said she'd never heard of him. John then asked if there were any more exhibits with pigs or hogs in Goliath Gardens. Again, the woman shook her head.

John walked away discouraged. He sighed, thinking his grandfather and uncle had been right after all. Coming to Goliath Gardens was probably useless.

John walked past more exhibits, watching carefully for any sign of the security guard. At the rear of the park, a whole new area had been opened up. A large arched sign was over the gate that led into the Goliath Garden of Delights. As John went inside, he felt less like a young man on a mission and more just like a kid on a Saturday afternoon in an amusement park. He thought less about his father, and more about having fun.

John wandered into the new section, staring up at the new and exciting attractions. He decided he would tour the area and then go on the rides that looked like the most fun. He walked slowly past the Faster Blaster Gallery (a kind of shooting gallery), The Living Doll House (a place where you played and made up like the dolls), Caves and Cobras Super Game (which went underground in make-believe caves), Bammer Vehicles (cars that crashed and shot things), Video Idiotville (a place of giant TV screens showing strange and unusual games and images) and Demonia Palace (a kind of spook house). But the one that caught his eye was right next to the Demonia Palace, the Super Heroes' Horrible House of Horrors.

An old, ugly, two-headed woman was talking inside a glass ball by the gate outside, urging people to go in. John walked up closer, trying to figure out how they managed to make the two-headed woman look so real. The sign below the two heads said, "Wanda and Wendy, the Mutant Two-Headed Lady. What's on both their minds?"

"Be a Super Hero in the House of Horrors!" one shouted out. "Step right up, young and old, today's your day to prove you're not afraid. To prove you have what it takes to battle such horrible and awful creatures as Belinda the Grave Lady, Crazy Joe the Hogman, Murdering Mike the Maniac, Jack the Ripper, Sludgeman, the Ax Killer, Z-Rax the Deadbot from the planet Avownia. Plus there's lots more. Come and face the worst and the most fearsome today. Kill them, blast them, knock them down, and if you're a good enough hero, you may get a bonus prize. Who will be the one who comes out wearing the Trophy Crown? Who will be the winner in the next group of heroes. Everyone's a hero, first, second and third class. Now's your chance. Come inside the Super Heroes' Horrible House of Horrors today and be a hero. Step right up. Don't miss your chance today."

John looked at the pictures outside the Horrible House of Horrors. All the monsters looked big and ugly and mean. The children came out of the exhibit talking excitedly.

"Did you see the way I blasted that old lady with my purple Slime Ball?" a little boy boasted.

"Look at my medal!" the other boy replied. "I got five direct hits. I really clobbered that Murdering Mike guy."

John Kramar moved closer. The other children pressed eagerly toward the line. He stared up at Wanda and Wendy.

"You aren't afraid, are you, boy?" the head named Wendy asked.

"He's a chicken, just like his old man," the other head said and began to laugh. "I bet you're afraid of little ole Lester! I bet you're a real coward!"

"I am not!" John replied. "I'm not afraid."

"Then why don't you go in?" Wendy asked. "Surely you want to prove you're a hero. Go inside the Super Heroes' Horrible House of Horrors and prove who you are."

John was about to say something when he saw the security guard walking in his direction. John wasn't sure whether the guard had seen him or not, but he didn't want to wait around and find out.

He ran quickly up the ramp. He glanced back. The guard seemed to be looking right at him. John turned away. Suddenly, the floor began to move and John began his journey through the Super Heroes' Horrible House of Horrors.

THE
HOGMAN

· · · · · · · ·

10

John figured the House of Horrors would be dark, but he hadn't guessed how strange and eerie the music would sound.

Far in the distance he could hear screams and shouts and yells. Like the other kids, he held onto the railing in front of him as the whole platform they stood on took them down deeper into the House of Horrors.

When the platform stopped, they were in a room full of heroes. Everywhere John looked were lifelike statues that talked. Some were actors in cowboy outfits like John Wayne and Clint Eastwood. Some were in military uniforms. Some were in fighting costumes. Some were women with swords and spears in their hands. Others were cartoon super heroes. They all looked strong and tough.

"Go for it, do it," the statues whispered. "Kill them. Make my day. Knock their blocks off."

"Go to your ammo booth and get your ammunition now," a loud-speaker said. "Your journey through the Super Heroes' House of Horrors will begin as soon as you choose your weapons."

The children got Lazer Guns and Faster Blasters, which shot paint pellets. But what everyone wanted were the rubbery Slime Balls, which resembled water balloons but were filled with gooey mud. John loaded up, grabbing as many of the Slime Balls as he could. Then they all got into little train cars that ran on a track into the rest of the House of Horrors.

The ride began. Immediately, John felt a stab of fear. He knew it was all pretend, but something inside him felt afraid when he heard the screams begin as they entered the darkness. A deep, echoing voice on a loudspeaker inside the cars began taunting the riders: "You won't go through with it. You're chicken," the voice said. "You won't open your eyes. You won't face *the Grave Lady!!!*"

The car was riding through a hillside that got dark and cold. Wind was blowing. Thunder and lightning crashed. They entered a forest.

"Back in a deep forgotten woods on the outside of a town, a group of children stumbled upon an old forgotten cemetery. . . ."

The train pulled around a sharp curve. John saw old trees and graves. With the cool air and the lightning, he suddenly began to feel more scared. Even though he knew it was pretend, everything seemed so real.

The cars moved slowly, creaking along. All the other kids were ready with their Lazer Guns.

"Grave robbers came out to the hidden cemetery to find old jewelry and gold," the voice said. "But they found more than they bargained for. . . ."

Suddenly, from out of a deep hole near a headstone, a woman popped up out of a casket. Like everyone else, John screamed in surprise and fear. Then the children began throwing the Slime Balls and shooting Faster Blaster paint pellets. The old woman shrieked as she was covered with brightly colored paint and gooey mud. John threw one of his Slime Balls as hard as he could but missed. The old woman in graveclothes disappeared down the hole and the train moved on.

The train came into a dark old farmyard. The wind still blew desolate and cool. A herd of large grunting mechanical pigs moved in a big puddle of slop and mud.

"Nobody's been farming out at the old place for years," the voice said. "But some say the old farmyard isn't abandoned after all. Sometimes you can hear Old Joe calling the hogs in the evening. But everyone knows Old Joe went crazy and died years ago . . . or did he?"

John braced himself; something sounded disturbingly familiar, but he couldn't figure out what it was. "He's been among the hogs so long, he's starting to look like them. They say he may not be human anymore. Watch out for the Hogman!"

And at that moment, a man with a pig snout burst out of a door with a bucket. John jerked back. The man, dressed in old clothes, snorted and yelled at the kids. The children screamed; then Slime Balls and Blaster pellets filled the air. John stood up in the car to throw his first Slime Ball. The man turned and faced John as the Slime Ball hit him squarely in the chest. As the goo and the mud dripped off his chest, John cocked his arm to throw another but stopped. Suddenly he remembered what his mother had said.

"Old Joe is calling the hogs every day. Some say he's a pig himself."

John looked at the pathetic man covered with mud in the pen of make-believe pigs. Then he realized what his mother was talking about.

"Dad?" John cried out. But the cars started to move on. "Dad? Joe Kramar?"

The Hogman turned and looked at the boy in the car pulling away.

Even with the mud on his face, John could tell that the man was listening.

"Dad, it's me!" John shouted. "I'm John Kramar, your son."

John could see the cars were pulling through a curtain toward the next exhibit. Without thinking, John pulled himself out of the car. He leaned against the wall in the dark as the other cars rolled away.

He ran back along the little track and stood in front of the exhibit. The man with the pig snout on his face looked at John without speaking.

"You're Joe Kramar, aren't you?" John asked. He could hardly believe what he saw. The man stared at John and wiped mud off his face. He said nothing. The mechanical pigs stopped squealing. In the dim light, John could hear the screams and the loud voices of children battling monsters and villains.

"Dad, it's me, John Kramar," the boy said. "I came to look for you. I want to bring you home. Mom is in the hospital. She's real sick. Dad, won't you come home?"

The man in the muddy shirt just stood looking at John. Then he stared down at his feet. He picked up his straw hat from the mud. Without looking back, he turned and started walking toward the mud house.

"Dad, it's me," John said softly. He voice cracked and his eyes filled with tears as he saw his father slip in the mud.

"Hold it right there, young man!" a voice said. John whirled around. In the dark was a hallway. Two men in gray ORDER uniforms came at John.

"No!" John shouted, and he threw the Slime Ball he was holding straight at one of the guards. The Slime Ball splatted against his chest. The guard looked surprised but kept coming.

"You're coming with me," the guard said.

"Dad!" John Kramar called out. "Don't let them take me! You've got to come home with me."

"Get back inside the shed, Joe," the other guard said. "It's Ernie's turn to come out, then Roscoe's. We'll take care of this boy."

"Dad, it's me, John Kramar, your son!" John shouted out. "Don't let them take me away. You've got to come with me!"

But the man with the pig's mask said nothing as they carried the yelling boy away.

John waited anxiously in the security lab room. He looked out the barred window. A carload of noisy riders went up the tall hill of the Goliath Three. As they zoomed down, some of the riders held their hands up in the air to show they were brave.

And maybe they were brave, John thought. Maybe everyone was brave except him. And his dad. John thought of his father again, standing in the knee-deep slop and mud, wallowing like a pig to amuse a trainload of children. Once again, John felt a wave of embarrassment and shame.

He looked down at his feet. His shoes were splattered with drops of mud. John stared at them, but all he could see was the pathetic face of a man among mechanical pigs.

"Nothing is working out like it's supposed to," he said softly to himself. John sat in silence, staring at his shoes, trying to understand how his father could be living the way he was living. The squealing of pigs still rang in the boy's ears.

An hour later the door opened. Grandfather Kramar and Uncle Bill walked into the room.

"John, are you all right?" Uncle Bill asked. He walked over quickly. "You gave us quite a scare running off like that."

"I'm okay," John said glumly. He looked up at the two men and then looked down at his shoes. He didn't know what to say, but he knew he had to tell them, even though he didn't want to.

"I found him," John blurted out. "I found Dad. . . ."

"He's here?" Uncle Bill asked.

John nodded his head up and down, afraid that he couldn't speak. His eyes were wet with tears.

"Where is he?"

"He's with the pigs," John choked out, and he began to sniffle. He bit his lip so he wouldn't cry.

"With the pigs?" Grandfather Kramar repeated.

"In the Super Heroes' Horrible House of Horrors," John said. Trying to hold back the sniffles, he related how he had found his father, standing knee deep in the mud.

"John, you wait here," Grandfather Kramar said. "Your uncle and I need to make a visit."

John nodded and sat back down. As the two men left the room, John wiped his eyes, trying to dry up every shred of evidence of what he was feeling.

Half an hour later, his grandfather and uncle returned to the small room. John wasn't surprised that they came alone.

"Did you see my father?" John asked.

"We saw where he works, but we didn't see him," Grandfather Kramar said. He frowned. "Apparently he didn't want to see us or someone didn't want him to see us."

"He wouldn't even talk to me," John said. "Not even one word."

"He must not be ready," Grandfather Kramar said.

"I haven't seen him in years, and he's not ready to talk?" John asked.

"John, we know you're upset," Uncle Bill said. "We better go home. There'll be other times to talk to your dad."

"What makes you think he'll talk to us then?" John asked bitterly. The two men were quiet for a moment.

"I think your uncle is right," Grandfather Kramar said. "We've all had a long day and need to get home."

"Goliath Gardens has decided not to press any charges against you," Uncle Bill said to John as they walked toward the door. "They just didn't want a runaway on their hands."

"I won't be back to bother them. They can be sure of that," John said firmly. Neither man responded.

The ride home seemed like the longest John had ever taken. He felt numb with tiredness. He pretended to sleep as his uncle drove through the darkness. Over and over again he saw his father knee deep in the mud, silent, then turning away. No matter how tightly he closed his eyes, he kept seeing the same scene.

Once they got home, John went quickly to the attic. He was surprised to see the light on. Then he saw Lester, Jr., sitting on another bed. A stack of John's comic books surrounded him.

"What are you doing?" John demanded.

"Can't you see, stupid?" Lester replied. "I'm reading comic books."

"But why are you up here?"

Before Lester could reply, John heard steps on the attic stairs. Uncle Bill's head popped up around the corner.

"We decided to move Lester, Jr., up here with you, John," Uncle Bill said. "Cousin Lester was too crowded. You boys both go to bed. It's too late to stay up and talk. Good night."

Uncle Bill went back down the stairs. John sat down on his bed.

"He can't tell me when to go to bed," Lester said. "He's not my dad."

"Well, I'm going to bed," John said. "Give me back my comic books. I didn't give you permission to read them."

John stood up and stepped forward. As he leaned down, his cousin whirled around and suddenly pushed John hard on the chest. Caught off balance, John sat down hard on the hard wooden floor. A sharp pain burned in his tailbone.

"I told you I wasn't ready for bed," Lester said defiantly. "Besides, my daddy said I could read these. I don't need your permission."

John scrambled to his feet. Lester leaped to his feet; his hands were now fists, ready. John stared at the bigger boy.

"Come on, you little wimp," Lester said. "You want to fight? I'll pound you right now."

Seeing the older boy's fists in the dim lonely light of the attic made John feel afraid. Then he felt disgusted and angry with himself because he was afraid. He wasn't sure what to do. The day had already been too long and had held too many disappointments.

"I'm going to bed," John said wearily. "We'll settle this tomorrow."

"I knew you were afraid to fight," Lester sneered. "Go hide in the bed, you little wimp."

John took a deep breath. He turned away, his face burning red. As he walked across the room, he heard Lester snickering. He buried himself totally under the covers so he wouldn't hear Lester turning the pages of the comic books. But hiding under the covers couldn't take away all the thoughts that chased the boy into his sleep.

THE
HOMELESS
FIND HOME
· · · · · · · ·
11

The next day, Sunday, John lay in his bed hoping he would never have to get up and face the day. But when Les, Jr., came upstairs after breakfast, he made no attempt to be quiet. He slammed drawers and hummed to himself.

"You better get up," Lester said. "They're having another big meeting of all the Spirit Flyer clubs today. Number Day is just a week away. Plus they're inviting those Garbage People too. I can smell them already. I don't know why your uncle insists on trying to be friends with those kind of lowlifes. My dad says they'll get us all in trouble for sure. I don't know why your uncle gets to make all the decisions. We should get to vote at least."

John sat up in his bed. He tried to shake the sleep out of his head. He rubbed his eyes.

"You got in pretty late last night," Lester said. "We didn't really have time to set the rules for being up here together."

"This is my room," John said sullenly.

"Well, it's my room now too, since Dad said it was too crowded in your room downstairs for both him and me," Lester, Jr., said defiantly. "And I've been thinking. I think I should be by the big window. After all, I am a guest in this house."

"But this bed weighs a ton," John grunted. "I don't want to move it."

"That's another thing," Lester replied. "I think I should have that bed instead of you. I don't like the little bed. Besides, it creaks when I turn over in the night."

"Let me get this straight," John said, trying not to get angry. "You want my bed and my window even though your stupid father already kicked me out of my own room before."

"You better watch your mouth unless you want a fat lip," Lester threatened. He took a step toward John, holding his fists up. John sat up straighter in his bed. Even though he was still sleepy he could see Lester meant business. John felt a stab of fear, not sure how to handle the bigger boy. Lester walked all the way over to John's bed. He looked down at John with contempt.

"I think we should ask Uncle Bill about it," John said feebly, though he didn't believe that would satisfy his cousin. And it didn't.

"No way," Les, Jr., said. "He'd just stick up for you. He's your uncle. I say we change beds tonight. After all, like I told you, I'm your guest."

Lester smiled a sweet mean smile. John looked away. He wanted to jump up and smash Lester in the face as hard as he could, but Lester would be waiting for a fight.

"You win," John said with a sigh. "If you want to switch, we'll switch. I'm not going to argue."

"I didn't think you would," Lester said with a smirk. "You really are a chicken, aren't you? Just like your ole man."

"What are you talking about?" John demanded.

"Don't act so surprised," Lester said. "I heard the whole story this morning at breakfast. Your uncle told everyone about your Hogman daddy. I could hardly believe it, but then, the more I think about it, the more it all makes sense. Like father, like son. No wonder he didn't want to show his face around Centerville. I'd rather be dead than let anyone see me like that. I went on that ride four times. I bet I must have hit your old man with a dozen Slime Balls myself."

A surge of anger welled up in John. For an instant he was ready to fight. But the anger turned to shame as the words sank in. Maybe he *was* like his father. That's what he had been secretly afraid of last night as he hid under the covers. Maybe he *was* a kind of freakish coward.

John didn't say anything as Les, Jr., moved his stuff. And when Les got his box of best comic books, John just walked down the steps without saying a word.

In the kitchen, John poured himself a bowl of cereal. Susan, Lois and Katherine were at the counter making bread. Each one had her own job. John was sure that they were staring at him. He knew that they had heard about his father at Goliath Gardens.

"I'm sorry the meeting with your dad didn't go well," Susan said as she greased a bread pan.

"That's the breaks," John said simply.

"Did he really look like a pig?" Katherine asked in her tiny voice.

"Ssshhhhh," Susan said to her sister.

"But that's what Daddy said," Katherine insisted.

"I know, but you don't have to—"

"It's OK," John said. "You guys don't have to pretend. I know what they told you. I just wish they hadn't told Les, Jr., too."

"Cousin Lester made such a fuss yesterday that Mom and Dad felt like they had to send Les, Jr., up in the attic with you," Susan said apologetically.

"He's taking over the place," John said. "But I don't care. I don't care in the least. Why should I?"

"I wouldn't want him in my room," Katherine said.

Everyone was quiet for a while. John ate while the girls worked on the bread. Susan seemed troubled.

"Is it true that your father didn't even get a chance to speak to you?" Susan asked finally.

"He had a chance," John said. "He just didn't take it. He didn't want me to come. I shouldn't have gone. It was a waste of money."

"Grandpa Kramar said they would go back," Lois said. "He said that your dad wouldn't talk to them either."

"I guess he doesn't have much to say," John replied. He took his empty bowl to the sink and rinsed it.

"We'll never get through with this baking," Susan said. "All the people at the dump are moving out here today."

"What?" John asked. "Les, Jr., mentioned that they were coming for some meeting, but not to stay."

"They're going to stay in the south pasture," Lois said. "It's going to be like a campground, Daddy says."

Aunt Betty walked into the kitchen. She came over and squeezed John by the shoulders.

"I hope you aren't too crowded up in the attic," Aunt Betty said. "You had already left when we decided to move Les, Jr. But Cousin Lester seemed so unhappy the way things were, we just thought you two boys would be better off sharing a room so Lester could be by himself."

"Les, Jr., doesn't know what *share* means," John said.

"Well, he'll have to learn if he stays around," Aunt Betty replied. She seemed busy. "We're all going to have to learn to share more after today."

"Are the people from the dump really moving out here?" John asked.

"Not all of them," Aunt Betty said. "Many have left the area since the ORDER people drove them out of the dump. This will be better for them anyway. Being so close to all that garbage just isn't healthy. Anyway, there's still a lot to do. Grandpa needs you to help him, John, as soon as you can. He's out in the workshop." John nodded. He went back upstairs. Without speaking to Les, Jr., he got dressed in his work clothes and went back downstairs.

John helped his grandfather mark off living areas along the south pasture road. They used string and wooden stakes to mark the boundaries of each campsite. His grandfather didn't say anything about John's dad, and John was grateful. The old man seemed preoccupied with getting things ready, though John wasn't sure that was it.

"Maybe he's disappointed like I am, but not saying anything," John thought. Even though John worked hard, his thoughts were back in Goliath Gardens. He wondered if his father was getting pelted by Slime Balls or falling down in the mud. John was glad there was plenty of work to do. It helped keep his mind off his father.

In the early afternoon, the people began arriving. They came on foot and in old cars and on bicycles. Some were carrying suitcases. Some were pushing wheelbarrows.

John was surprised there were so many people needing a place to live. The Kramar family stood by the workshop and watched them arrive. Grandfather Kramar and Uncle Bill greeted them.

"We'll make as much room for them as we can," Grandfather Kramar said. "We have more than enough space along the south pasture road. We've rented some portable toilets for sanitation."

"How can we help all these people, Mama?" Lois asked.

"By giving them a place to stay," Mrs. Kramar replied. "One thing we have is space. At least for now. Your father and Grandpa will put a water line in. People can cook and eat. It's not the best situation, but it will be better than all the flies and garbage out at the dump. They can't call them Garbage People now."

"I think it's exciting," Susan said. "We can have a regular school now, and not just a home school."

"The other parents will have to help out, especially since I've got little Paul Nathaniel to look after," Mrs. Kramar said. "But we can manage, I suppose. Things could be a lot worse. The kings will provide what we need. All we need to provide is the love."

"There sure are a lot of them," Lois said in her small voice. "I think we should call them the Pasture People, not the Garbage People."

Mrs. Kramar laughed and patted her on the back. "I think that's a splendid name for them," she said. They all watched as the rows of people kept coming.

Later that evening, in the field just south of the workshop, the people with Spirit Flyers were gathering in a large circle.

"Everyone looks so serious," Lois said. Susan nodded.

"We all knew Number Day was coming," Mrs. Kramar said. "But it's still a shock. I didn't believe the government would really go through with it. It's hard to believe it's really happening."

"My mother's really upset," Daniel Bayley said solemnly. "I had to beg her to let me come today. She still thinks I'll get into more trouble because I have a Spirit Flyer."

John kept to himself more than usual. He stood on the outside of the circle. He moved farther away from the people with the Spirit Flyer bicycles as they began to sing songs to the kings. He just didn't have a song in his heart. He felt as if he'd never sing again. He walked toward the house. The light in the attic was on, which probably meant Lester, Jr., was up there.

John sighed. Another traveler was coming up the driveway. John shook his head. He didn't see how there could be more people still coming.

As the person got closer, John could see that it was a man with dark hair. Then John looked more intently. Something seemed familiar about this man. John walked toward the driveway. As the man got closer and closer, something about him made John feel uneasy. Then he saw his face more clearly. John gasped.

The man coming up the driveway was his father.

THE
LOST SON
RETURNS
· · · · · · · ·
12

John ran to his father. Joe Kramar stopped.
John hugged him excitedly, but his father hardly hugged him back. John
tried not to notice how his father seemed like a total stranger.

"You came back, you came back!" John cried. "I knew you wouldn't
leave us this way, I knew you had to come home!"

Some others nearby began to notice the commotion. Grandfather
Kramar and Uncle Bill moved away from the circle of singers. Grandfather squinted at John and the strange man.

"I believe that's Joe," Grandfather Kramar said. The old man ran to
his son. For a moment it was three generations of Kramars hugging, with

John squeezed in the middle of the two men.

John noticed his Uncle Bill walking more slowly toward them. Cousin Lester was right behind him.

Bill Kramar walked over and stuck out his hand toward his brother. For the first time in years, the two brothers shook hands.

"You've kept up the place real well, Bill," Joe said. "And I want to thank you for taking care . . . of everything."

John was surprised to see that his uncle didn't look so happy to see his own brother. Uncle Bill looked uneasy more than anything. He stared at his brother. Cousin Lester frowned as he looked down his long thin nose.

"This calls for a real celebration," Grandfather Kramar said, his face beaming at his son. "We'll have the biggest barbecue and party this old farm has ever seen."

"A party?" Joe Kramar asked softly, as if he couldn't believe his ears. "Dad, I've made a lot of bad mistakes, and I have a lot to tell you. I hardly know where to start. I don't expect any favors or special treatment. I was hoping I could come back and work as a hired hand around here, if there's work to do on the farm."

"Hired hand? Nonsense!" Grandfather Kramar said. "You're my son and this was your farm! But first we have to have a celebration. You're back. It's like my dead son has come back to life."

Joe Kramar didn't say anything. His eyes were suddenly wet with tears. He looked down at his feet.

"Everything will be OK now that you're back," John said. "We'll have to go tell Mom. She's real sick."

"Mary is here?" Joe asked in surprise.

"She's in the hospital in Kirksville," Grandfather Kramar said. "It looks very serious. Come, let me show you what we've done with the place since you've been gone. We'll tell you about Mary too. Wait till your mother hears you're home! She's up at our place with Aunt Thelma."

Grandfather Kramar had his arm around Joe as they walked toward the crowd of people gathered behind the workshop. John ran along beside them.

"Are you coming, Uncle Bill?" John called out.

"In a while," Uncle Bill replied, taking a deep breath.

Cousin Lester walked over to Uncle Bill. The tall thin man shook his head from side to side.

"Can you believe it?" Cousin Lester asked.

"We all thought he and Mary were dead for sure," Uncle Bill said. "It's still hard to get used to the idea that both of them are alive after all this time."

"But can you believe he had the nerve to come home?" Cousin Lester asked. "Gone for years, then poof! He comes home and wants everyone to throw him a party. Right before Number Day no less. It's easy to see why he came back. Probably got fired from his job and is looking for a handout like all these other people."

"It's all so sudden and strange, isn't it?" Uncle Bill said.

"More than strange," Cousin Lester said. "I don't want to say anything against your family, but this brother of yours seems like a moocher and a sponge. A fair-weather friend showing up at the last minute. Yet your father is treating him like a regular hero or something. You've been here all these years, taking care of business and working hard; then out of the blue, here comes your brother asking for handouts, without a word of explanation as to where he's been for years or why he abandoned his own child."

"Maybe so," Bill Kramar said, nodding his head. "Well, if Dad wants a party, he's going to need some help. We better get after it."

"Hmmphft!" Cousin Lester said. "I don't think I'd lift a finger to help a brother like that."

And he didn't. But the party went on. There were barbecue and hamburgers and hot dogs for everyone, not to mention the beans and potato salad and loaves of hot toasty bread, sliced and buttered and sprinkled with garlic.

Long makeshift tables were made by putting boards and old doors on sawhorses. The food was set out and the people lined up. Aunt Betty, Susan, Lois and John helped serve the food as the people came through the line, while Katherine watched little Paul Nathaniel. Grandfather Kramar and his son Joe went through the line first.

"I want to thank the kings that my son who was lost has now been found," Grandfather Kramar announced. "I can't say how surprised and happy I am. So I'm throwing this party in honor of his return."

Everyone clapped except Cousin Lester and Uncle Bill. They stood by the big barbecue grill where John's uncle helped cook the meat.

"I'm just glad to be back," John's father said. "Thank you for this welcome."

Everyone held hands while Grandfather Kramar gave thanks for the food. When he finished, the people clapped.

"Let's eat!" Grandfather Kramar shouted, and the feast began.

Later, Bill Kramar was cleaning the grill. Cousin Lester came over to watch. It was dark, and most of the people had gone to their tents and trailers.

"Your brother certainly seems to have enjoyed himself," Cousin Lester said. "Your father is a kind man and very generous, but I'm afraid he's going to carry this generosity stuff too far. We only have limited resources on this farm. We can't feed the whole world, let alone some Johnny-come-lately long-lost son who shows up at the last minute before times really get tight on Number Day."

"He did show up at the right time, I guess," Uncle Bill said. "He looks tired, doesn't he?"

"He looks like a man who knows how to mooch, if you ask me," Cousin Lester replied. "Of course, no one listens to me around here. I've seen characters like him before. For all we know, he could be a spy. And how does he account for himself? Gone all this time. You've sacrificed all these years raising his child. And as soon as he gets back, your father acts like he's ready to give him the keys to the whole place again."

"This used to be his farm," Bill said slowly. "But with him gone, it went to John and to us because we were John's legal guardians."

"Well, I don't want to tell anyone what to do, but I'd watch this bird real closely," Cousin Lester said. "The whole thing sounds like a big complicated lawsuit in the making. I'd get a lawyer working on this tonight. No telling what your brother's intentions are. Imagine, just walking in here like he owned the place and not a word of explanation as to where he's been or why he was gone. Not one word of explanation."

"He'll tell us the whole story when he's ready, I reckon," Bill said. "At least I assume he will. I mean he does owe us that much."

"He owes a lot more than that, I'd say," Cousin Lester sniffed. "I'm just afraid your father isn't exercising good judgment. Some people lose their common sense when it comes to their families, especially their children."

"Sometimes I think my dad had a blind spot when it came to Joe," Uncle Bill said sourly. "Joe always was something of a dreamer. For instance, he left a perfectly good teaching job to run a toy store. He had a good heart, but you have to have common sense too. The business was as risky as they come. But you couldn't tell him anything. He was determined to do it. I remember my dad encouraged him in that little enterprise."

"I know what you mean," Cousin Lester said with a nod. "You see, some fathers have blind spots when it comes to their own children, especially if they are the favored ones . . ."

"My dad never said Joe was the favorite," Uncle Bill said defensively.

"Maybe not in words," Cousin Lester said, "but what about in actions? Did your dad ever throw a big party for you all these years? You've been here taking care of business, working hard, but did you ever get a hero's welcome and a feast to boot?"

"Well, no, not really," Uncle Bill replied.

"Actions sometimes speak louder than words is all I'm saying, not that anyone listens to me."

"He did put on a really good feast for everyone," Uncle Bill said. He picked up a wire brush to wipe across the grill.

"An appalling display of unfairness and favoritism, I think," Cousin Lester said. He reached down to the table and picked up a leftover pickle from a jar. "Of course, you can make up your own mind. I'm just an outside observer."

Behind the two men, in the shadows of the workshop eaves, Joe Kramar was listening to his brother and Cousin Lester. He hadn't said a word. In the moonlight, his face looked paler than usual. He bowed his head sadly and backed up further into the shadows, leaving Bill and Cousin Lester to talk.

THE BIGGEST
FOOL IN
CENTERVILLE
· · · · · · · ·

13

When John Kramar woke up the next morning, the first thing he saw was a set of golden keys on a large key ring on his bedpost. "The keys," John said softly. "Why do I keep seeing them? I don't have any use for them."

As soon as he said that, the keys were gone, if they had ever even been there. Sometimes John thought he was just dreaming or seeing things. All night long he had dreamed about his father. In his dreams his father almost seemed asleep or something worse, as if he were drunk or had been using some drug. He kept grabbing his father's face and was trying to make him talk. But all his father would do was moan. John would reach up and move his father's lips, but he still couldn't get him to talk. In the dream, his father's lips felt fake and rubbery, as if his face were all a mask. John woke up, trying to get his father to break the silence.

John got dressed quickly, anxious to go down and talk to his father. Even though he was glad for his father to be home, part of him still felt very strange about the whole situation. In fact, he was surprised at how he felt. He thought he should feel really happy like Grandfather Kramar, but John didn't feel that way.

He wasn't sure why, but he felt embarrassed. He wondered what Amy and his other friends would think when they found his father had been working as Crazy Joe the Hogman. No matter how he tried to think about it, he couldn't avoid the ugly feelings of being embarrassed.

John had always dreamed that his father would be heroic. But in the flesh, he seemed much more quiet and sad than John had imagined. John had always pictured his father as strong and decisive, like Uncle Bill, especially since they were brothers. But his father seemed, for lack of a better word, weak.

"Maybe he was just tired from the long trip," John told himself as he put on his socks. "Or maybe he's sick. I'll bet he'll feel better today." As soon as he thought of his father being sick, John remembered his mother in the hospital. A wave of worry passed over the boy. Surely his dad wasn't as sick as his mother. For a moment, John wondered if his dad had a problem with Traginite-Z, like his mother.

That made John even more anxious. He finished dressing in a rush. He pulled up the sheet on his bed, then opened the attic door. He ran down the steps and burst into the kitchen.

His aunt and uncle and grandfather were sitting at the table drinking coffee. Cousin Lester was buried in the morning newspaper. Everyone looked at John quietly. For a moment, John thought he had done something wrong.

"I thought Dad would be here eating with you all," John said eagerly. "Is he up yet?"

"Your father slept in the workshop last night, we think," Grandfather Kramar said. "We offered him a bed in the house, but I guess he didn't feel worthy or something. I'm not even sure he slept here at all. When I went out to the shop this morning, I found this note."

Grandfather Kramar gave John a piece of paper and John read it.

Dear Dad, Bill and John,

I had a lot of doubts about whether or not I should have come home. I appreciate the fine dinner and all you've done, but I think it's just better if I stay away. A long time ago I made some bad mistakes and decisions. I feel like I've lost my rights to be a part of this family. I don't deserve your kindness. It would have been better for all concerned if I had stayed away forever. I know I've let everyone down, now for a second time. I don't want to make it any worse, so it's best that I should go and you forget all about me. I will try to have money transferred to your account when I get any extra to help take care of John and Mary. Goliath Gardens sends out a traveling carnival each spring. I'll go with them. I'm sorry I disappointed you all.

Joe.

John read through the paper a second and a third time. He felt his face getting hot. His eyes filled with tears. He sat down. He put the note on the table. The room was quiet. Cousin Lester turned a page of the paper.

"I don't know why any of you are surprised," Cousin Lester said. "I had a feeling he wouldn't stay. Some men just can't face up to their responsibilities in this life. They just cause trouble for the rest of us."

John nodded his head slowly. For the first time, he realized he agreed with Cousin Lester about something.

"It would have been better if he hadn't come back," John said, his voice shaking. "All he wanted to do was hurt everyone."

"John, you don't mean that," Aunt Betty said. She put her hand on his shoulder, but John shook it off.

"Yes, I do," the boy said. "I wish he had just stayed away. I wish he had died in that storm." His voice grew louder. "I wish they both had died. They didn't care about me or anyone else. They would both be better off dead!"

John stood up and ran out of the room and down the back steps, sobbing and saying over and over, "I wish they were dead. I wish they were dead."

After several minutes, he seemed to have exhausted himself. He stood motionless for some time except for the heaving of his chest. Soon he was breathing normally. Outside in the morning sunshine, he suddenly felt in control of himself. He wiped his eyes. His hands were clenched into fists.

Susan and Grandfather Kramar came down the back steps. They walked slowly toward John.

"I'm OK now," John said. "You don't have to worry about me. I'm not going to cry anymore for either one of them."

Grandfather Kramar looked very sad as he stared at John. Susan stood awkwardly beside the old man, unsure of what to say.

"Some people have good parents. Some people don't," John said. "I was just one of those kids who had lousy parents. Like he said, he made a bunch of bad decisions. He was right—he shouldn't have come home. I don't know why I even bothered to look for him. It was all a waste of time and money. I was a lot better off without them. I hope I never see him or her as long as I live."

John spat on the ground and walked quickly toward the workshop. He flung open the door. All the Spirit Flyer bicycles were in the room. John grunted when he saw his bike.

"I should have listened to you," John snarled at the old bicycle. "You warned me not to go. I shouldn't have tried to see either one of them."

"But your Spirit Flyer did help you save your mother," Susan said. She stood in the doorway. Grandfather Kramar was behind her.

"It was all one big mistake," John grunted. "If I hadn't given her a ride, I wouldn't have gotten into any of this mess. I wish I had left her on that road."

"She might have died, though," Susan replied. "You may have saved her life."

"She's dying anyway, isn't she? It didn't do any good. I was a fool for even trying, for even hoping. I was the biggest fool in Centerville to believe in either one of them. I'm never going to trust anyone again."

John walked over to the corner where his father had left the sleeping bag and mat. He bent down and began folding the sleeping bag. After it was folded, he rolled it up and tied the strings. He carried the sleeping bag over to a shelf by the window and set it down.

"We won't need that anymore," John said simply.

"John, I know you're disappointed in your mom and dad," Grandfather Kramar said softly. "I'm disappointed too. Very disappointed. I wish none of this had happened. They caused you and your aunt and uncle a lot of pain. They've caused your old grandma and me a lot of pain too. But when I saw your daddy coming up the drive, I had hope for the first time in years that a bad situation was about to turn around."

"You were a fool for hoping too," John spat out. He was sorry the minute he said it because he sounded so angry and disrespectful. Susan gasped. Grandfather Kramar walked over and stood in front of John. John looked up and then began to turn and walk away defiantly. But before he took a step he felt a big hand on his shoulder. In an instant, he was spinning around. The old man had a strength the boy had never realized or experienced.

"Young man, don't you ever call me a fool again," Grandfather Kramar said. John felt as if the old man's eyes would stare holes right through him.

"But he left me!" John cried out. All the controlled anger John had held up to that point was suddenly gone. He fell into his grandfather's arms and began to sob again. "I hate him. I hate her. All they want to do is hurt us."

John blubbered and cried. His grandfather just held him. When John opened his eyes, he saw the golden keys again through blurry eyes. They were hanging on the handlebars of his Spirit Flyer. The old man patted John on the back.

"John, the kings are calling you to do one of the hardest things in this life," the old man said.

"What's that?" sniffled John.

"To love someone even though it hurts to do it," Grandfather Kramar replied. "Some people are hurting so bad with all their problems that it's hard for us to love them, even when love is what they need the most."

"But I can't love him," John wailed. "He left me. They both left all of us."

"There's more to it than that," the old man said. "Your father and mother made some mistakes, and they suffered for it. It's been a tragedy. Years have gone by and been lost. Your dad shared some with me. I've hardly ever seen a man so eaten up with shame and sorrow. He couldn't even look me in the eye once. That's why he left. He didn't leave because he didn't love you. I think he was afraid that no one could ever love him again, after all the mistakes he made."

"But he's acting like a coward!" John blurted out. "You threw a party for him. You welcomed him back. And he just goes away again."

"We didn't all welcome him back," Uncle Bill said. John whirled around. His uncle was standing in the door, his eyes wet with tears. John was surprised. He couldn't remember ever seeing his uncle come close to crying.

"What do you mean?" John asked.

"I mean, I've been struggling with the same thoughts and feelings you have," Uncle Bill said. "Joe is my brother and part of me was glad to see him. But another part of me was angry and unforgiving. Dad welcomed him back, but I didn't. I'm still angry that he left this morning. But I wish he was here so we could talk this whole thing out."

Grandfather Kramar looked at his older son. He walked over and hugged him. In his arms, Bill Kramar too began to sob.

"I should have told him I loved him," Bill whispered. "I didn't even say I was glad to see him."

Both John and Susan stared at the two men. Susan's eyes filled with tears as she watched her father. John didn't say anything. He wiped his nose with his sleeve. He felt as if a storm were churning up inside. He didn't know if he wanted to cry or be angry. Most of all he didn't want to be feeling anything. He wished he could turn off the painful burning flood of feelings inside. But he couldn't.

"We've all made mistakes," Grandfather Kramar said. He patted Bill on the back. His oldest son nodded and wiped his eyes. Grandfather then looked at John. "Your parents aren't the only ones. We all make mistakes and have been bound up in our chains. That's why the Kingson had to come and set us free. This whole situation with your parents has been tragic. But a bigger tragedy would be to have your father continue in his shame and stay away from home. Deep down, don't you wish he were back?"

John didn't answer. He took a deep breath. His anger and pride told him not to answer.

"I wish he were here," the old man said with a sigh. "More than almost anything I wish he was sitting at the dinner table right now in the kitchen. I don't care what he's done. He's still my son. And he's still your father."

"But he left us," John protested feebly.

"He made some tragic mistakes," his grandfather agreed, nodding his head. "But except for the help of the Kingson, we'd all end up in the chains of our shame, locked in fear and darkness. We're all imperfect people, saved by the love of the kings. We all have to learn how to love people who make mistakes. Isn't that what you want them to do for you?"

John didn't answer. Part of him wanted to believe his grandfather and part of him wanted to remain angry.

"We all needed the kings to free us from our chains and locks," the old man said. "You had that chance and everyone gets that chance. And sometimes, we need a second chance or even a third. Sometimes a man falls down and can't get up by himself. He needs someone to help him."

"What do you think I should do?' John asked. "How can I help my father? He doesn't even want help."

Suddenly, the sound of a blowing horn filled the front room of the workshop. John ran over to his bike.

"My Spirit Flyer!" John said excitedly. The old bike began to roll toward the boy as the sound of the horn grew louder. John had heard the mysterious old horn blow before a number of times, but it had always sounded like a warning . . . Now the horn sounded like many trumpets, a roaring royal blast that made one think a very important person was about to be introduced.

The whole room filled with music and light. John's knees shook and faltered, and the next thing he knew, he was on the cement floor of the workshop with the rest of his family. And standing in the middle of the room was the Prince of Kings himself.

JUDGMENT
· · · · · · · ·
14

The blast of trumpets finally stopped, though the music seemed to linger in the air like the smell of a fragrant perfume. No one spoke in the presence of the Kingson. John looked up from the ground. Just seeing him filled John with a sudden rush of joy and energy. The boy's sorrow seemed to disappear as the darkness disappears when a light is switched on. Grandfather Kramar, Susan and Uncle Bill all stared at the Kingson, waiting in the silence.

The Kingson looked first at Uncle Bill, then turned his head and looked at John. There was something very sobering about his look. John sensed an uneasiness rising up inside himself. In fact, the more the

Kingson stared at him, the more uneasy John became. John began to feel like someone who's been trying to hide what he did wrong and suddenly has discovered he can't hide it anymore.

"What . . . did . . . I . . . do?" John stammered. But as soon as he asked the question, he knew the answer, or at least part of it.

"What have we done?" Uncle Bill asked, as he bowed before the Kingson. John glanced at his uncle, who seemed to look like a boy, too, before the mighty king. He must make all men seem like little boys when he's around, John thought. The Kingson's gaze pierced right through them.

"Give it up," the Kingson said solemnly to both John and Uncle Bill. His eyes almost seemed to blaze as he focused on them. He didn't really seem angry, but you knew he meant business, John thought. "You've taken the rod of judgment, my rod, and presumed to use it as your own, as if you yourselves were kings. Give it back."

The Kingson turned to face Uncle Bill. John had never seen his uncle unable look anyone in the eyes, but this time was different. His uncle looked down under the convicting stare of the Prince of Kings.

"I have . . . I have judged my own brother," Uncle Bill stammered uneasily. "I admit it, Your Majesty. And I'm so sorry. I'll never do it . . . I mean, I will try never to do it again . . . please forgive me."

Uncle Bill snuffled like a boy in front the king. The Kingson smiled, but only for an instant. He then turned back to John.

Suddenly John wished he were anywhere else in the whole world. But he knew it wouldn't matter because the Kingson would have found him no matter where he was hiding. Part of John was grateful for knowing that was true, but he was still afraid to return the gaze of the Kingson. The longer he waited, the worse he felt.

"Stand up," the Kingson said. John immediately got to his feet. He looked once into the Kingson's eyes, then back down at the floor.

"You have not honored your parents as they deserve," the Kingson said softly. "And you, too, have presumed upon my throne, making yourself the judge of others."

"But they didn't act right," John suddenly blurted out. Though his voice shook, he felt anger rising up inside himself. "They left me, and never told anyone. They abandoned me and left me on my own. How can I honor them when they act like that? Why should I honor them? They hurt me. They gave me up."

"You are not their judge," the Kingson said sadly. "And they deserve honor not for what they do, but for who they are, your parents. When you honor them, you honor me. And when you dishonor them, I am dishonored."

Suddenly John felt very afraid. His knees began to feel very weak.

"As you judge another, so you are judged," the Kingson said. "Do you wish for me to judge you according to the same standards by which you've judged your parents? Or do you wish to release them to my judgment?"

John's fear increased. He realized that the Kingson was really offering him a choice. The boy suddenly fell forward, grabbing the Kingson's legs.

"I'm sorry, I'm sorry," John blurted out. "I won't do it again. Show me what I need to do."

In his shivering, John felt the firm hand of the Kingson on his head. When his hand lifted, John felt as if a great burden had been lifted off his whole body, as if a very heavy dark coat had been removed. He suddenly felt free and empty of the ugly, yucky feelings inside his stomach.

"You are forgiven," the Kingson said. "And I am pleased."

"But what do I do now?" John asked. Something was nagging the boy deep inside. The Kingson seemed to be waiting. Then John knew. He felt it in his pocket. John reached in and pulled out the black shiny number card. He held it up for everyone to see. Susan seemed especially surprised to see the card, but she wisely said nothing.

"You were still tasting the judgment you had passed on others," the

Kingson said. "Judgments taste bitter in the mouth, don't they?"

"Yes," John said softly.

"I accused them of compromising while I was making my own compromises. I took the number card when I knew I shouldn't."

"You have understood clearly," the Kingson said with a smile. "These schemes to avoid the pain of mistakes only draw it out longer." He took the number card from John's hand. In an instant, the card evaporated in a puff of black smoke.

"Thank you," John said with relief.

No sooner had he had spoken than his old red Spirit Flyer bicycle rolled forward. The golden keys rested on the handlebars.

"You have another journey to make," the Kingson said. "You would have made this journey at a different time if you had waited for me to send you. But when people send themselves, they miss the timetable of purposes and my Kingdom. Shortcuts will only make you lost."

John nodded. He could hear his grandfather's words, "shoes before socks," as soon as the Kingson had spoken.

"But what are the keys for?" John asked.

"You'll know when to use them," the Kingson replied.

John got on the old bicycle. He touched the ring of golden keys. The jingling noise they made reminded him of a wind chime.

"The keys sing their own song when they are needed," the Kingson said. "Go now. I am sending you."

The bicycle began to roll at once by itself. John held on tighter as he rolled for the door and then outside.

He hadn't gone three feet before the big front tire lifted up off the ground as the bike headed up into the sky. As the back tire left the ground, the bike shot upward. John hung on tightly to the handlebars.

In a few seconds, John was high up in the air, just beneath the clouds. Down below, the house and workshop and barn looked like tiny toys. Grandfather Kramar and Susan and Uncle Bill looked up and waved to him. Before John could return the wave, the old red Spirit Flyer soared into a curve and then straightened up as it headed south. John held on tighter as the wind rushed by his face. The wheels seemed to hum, and the bike sped even faster. The humming sound grew louder. Then there was a whirl and a whoosh, and the bike seemed to leap forward in the deep blue sky.

For a moment, everything was a blur of blue sky and white cloud. Time seemed to either pass extremely quickly or stand still. John was filled with excitement and anticipation. The old bike then suddenly shot back into a normal sky and slowed down.

John took a deep breath. Up ahead he saw the tall mountains of the Goliath Three roller coaster. The Spirit Flyer had taken him to the outskirts of Goliath Gardens.

"We're going to find my father, aren't we?" John whispered to the old bicycle.

As if to answer, the Spirit Flyer swooped down, sailing right under the tallest tower of the roller coaster. John held on tighter as the bike passed over into the Goliath Garden of Delights. The Spirit Flyer touched down softly and rolled to a stop in front of the Super Heroes' Horrible House of Horrors. None of the children seemed to notice him as the line poured into the dark spook house. Wanda and Wendy, the two-headed ticket taker, did notice, however. When they saw the Spirit Flyer, both of their brightly painted mouths fell open.

"You can't take that awful bike in there!" Wanda cried.

"Call the guards!" shouted Wendy.

"Help!" screamed Wanda. "There's a troublemaker on the loose."

The Spirit Flyer bike rose up into the air and headed straight for the doors of the House of Horrors. Wanda and Wendy were still screaming when John entered the darkness. The old bicycle followed the path of the train tracks that carried the children through the spook house.

The boy and bicycle passed over their heads as they pelted the Grave Lady. They were so busy yelling and throwing that only one person looked up.

"Hey, there's a boy on a bike," she said, but John had disappeared into the darkness.

The Spirit Flyer floated down and stopped in front of the old farmhouse. The big balloon tires hung in the air over the mud pile.

"Dad! I've come to get you," John shouted out. "Dad, I'm here. It's me, John."

The door of the farmhouse creaked open. Joe Kramar appeared in his dirty old farmer's clothes, with the rubber pig snout attached to his face.

"John, you shouldn't be here," he said. "Go on home, now. The kids will be here any second."

"I don't care," John said. "I want you to come home with me."

"I can't, son. I just can't," Joe Kramar said. He turned away sadly and headed back toward the farmhouse door.

"You have to come home!" John yelled. He jumped off the bike into the mud hole. The slippery ooze came up over his knees.

In the distance, John could hear the next carload of children coming. The loudspeaker blared out.

"Dad, please come home," John said.

Joe Kramar turned. As he did, the big mechanical pigs began to move and squeal as the first car came into sight.

"Watch out for Crazy Joe the Hogman!" Suddenly, the air was filled with flying Slime Balls.

"Dad!" John screamed. A Slime Ball knocked him off his feet. He fell face down in the slop and mud.

Joe Kramar turned to reach for his son. The whole place was filled with the noise of screaming children and the loudspeaker's taunts. Slime Balls shot through the air.

Joe Kramar slipped and fell in the mud hole. The children screamed with delight as the Slime Balls rained down. No one seemed to notice or care that John was in the scene. He was just another target to them. Slipping and sliding in the mud hole with his father only a few feet away, John felt a wave of shame. What would his friends think if they saw him like this, slipping around in the mud hole? John reached out once more toward his father, but fell down.

In the midst of the confusion, John looked deep into his father's eyes. Behind the ugly pig snout, he clearly saw for the first time both the shame and sorrow in his father's face. His father was embarrassed that John was down in the mud with him. Both father and son tried to get to their feet, but the pounding Slime Balls kept them off balance. Then the pounding stopped. The train cars of children had moved on into the darkness.

John tried to stand up again, but whole place began to shake. The mud hole bubbled and swirled. John reached out for his dad's hand, but slipped and fell.

"What's happening?" John cried out.

"You've got to get out now!" his father shouted. "Run away and never come back!"

The mud began to swirl in a circle, slowly at first and then faster and faster like water going down a drain. Both man and boy were pulled around and around in the whirlpool of slop and mud. John reached up and grabbed the tire of his Spirit Flyer. He tried to grab his father's hand as he was pulled around, but his father was going downward now. The swirling mud hole pulled him away.

"Dad!" John screamed. John clung to the old bicycle. Then he grabbed the key ring and held the ring out for his father to see if he could grab hold. His father lifted up an arm, but the pull of the mud hole was stronger. He missed the ring. With a heavy burping sound, the mud hole sucked his father under, so that only his hand was left above the mud. John let go of the Spirit Flyer wheel and leaped toward his father's hand. He grabbed his father's wrist as it disappeared under the mud.

"Help me!" John cried out, holding onto his father's hand. But the swirling mud pulled John down with his father. John yelled out once more before the sucking mud hole drowned out his scream and took him all the way under.

THE
PITY
PIT
· · · · · · · · ·
15

For an instant, John felt as if he would suffocate. He felt not so much as if he were falling, but as if he were being sucked deeper and deeper into the center of the earth. The darkness was absolute. He felt wet and cold and slippery. Finally he stopped going down, and he hit a great pool of dark muck with a splat.

John stood up. He wiped his eyes and spit out the muck. The golden ring of keys was still in his right hand. John pulled the big ring up his arm, up to his shoulder, where it stayed. When he looked around, he was surprised that he could see. They seemed to be inside a round room of some kind, though it was hard to tell since the light was so dim.

Everything was covered in mud and slop. There was a muddy bed, and a slop-covered chair and even a dresser with a mud-covered lamp on top. There were no doors or windows. Above them, the darkness hovered like a cloud.

Over by the muddy bed, his father was on his knees. He was just looking down into the mucky pool of mud on the floor.

"Dad? Are you all right?" John asked. He slogged over in the mud toward his father. The whole place had a stale, almost suffocating smell. There wasn't any fresh air.

"I shouldn't have brought you here," Joe Kramar mumbled softly to his son.

"What?" John asked.

"I shouldn't have tried to go home," his father said. "I knew it would lead to no good. I only mess things up."

"But where are we?"

Joe Kramar got to his feet. He shuffled across the muddy floor and turned on a muddy lamp. An eerie dim gray light came from the lamp.

"Joe Kramar!" a loud voice called. The voice came from above in the darkness.

"We've got to obey it," Joe said. "We can't resist."

"Resist what?" John asked. But as soon as he said it, his father was yanked forward and fell face down in the mud. Loud laughing filled the air. His father tried to get up again, but almost as soon as he stood, he was yanked again and fell. John ran to his father.

"Hold onto me," John said. He lifted his father by the arms. As he did, John saw the muddied dark chain attached to his father's waist.

"Joe Kramar!" the voice yelled.

His father was pulled again. This time he looked up into the darkness above him.

"It's too late, John. It's too late," his father said wearily, out of breath. "You shouldn't have come here."

Then out of the darkness above, a four-foot-square platform descended.

Peering over the edge of the platform was a large figure of a man that looked just like his father, only he wasn't muddy. He wore gray clothes. A rubbery pig snout covered his nose. In his hands he held a bucket. Using a rope, he lowered the bucket to Joe Kramar. John's father took the bucket and unfastened the rope. The bucket was filled with slop.

"Thank you, Master," Joe Kramar said.

"You stay in this pity pit, you pitiful pig!" the man with the pig's face said. Then he looked at John. The eyes glowed red with anger. "Now that brat with you can hear with his own ears all the disgusting things you've done."

John's father took the bucket of slop and lifted it up over his head, then poured it all down on himself. John watched in horror as the slop dripped down his father's face. The figure on the platform ascended slowly into the darkness, laughing as it disappeared.

"I told you not to come here," his father said in a monotone. "You don't want to see me like this."

"You don't live here?" John asked. The whole idea seemed impossible.

"I'm just brought here when I need to be punished," his father said. "Goliath Gardens only keeps the bad people in their pits."

"But you aren't a bad person," John said.

"I'm a terrible person," his father said. "Why else would I be here? This is for the bad people. That's why they come to visit."

"Who comes to visit?" John asked.

"Lots of people," his father said glumly. "Sometimes it seems like everyone I ever knew."

His father sat back in the bed and leaned against the wall. He looked sadly at John. Then he looked away as if embarrassed.

Suddenly they heard laughter and then just voices, as if out of nowhere. They filled the room. Whispering voices.

"He's afraid. He's a coward," the voices said, followed by more cruel laughter.

"He really messed up this time," said another voice in the darkness.

"What do you expect? He always messes up! He can't do anything right. He's a regular moron."

"He's lazy."

"He's stupid."

"He'll never get it right."

"You're running out of money. What an awful provider! You can't take care of business like everyone else."

"You should have done this."

"You should have done that."

"What kind of man are you?"

"What kind of husband and father are you?"

"You're pathetic."

"You disgust me so much I just want to throw up."

"He betrayed the kings for a bunch of money. He sold the Spirit Flyers for a few measly dollars. Where's that money now, Mr. Deal Maker?"

And then the faces came. In shimmering forms, on the walls of the muddy pit of a room, John saw faces. They seemed to be staring right at them.

One face looked just like Cousin Lester. He frowned as he spoke.

"He looks like a man who knows how to mooch, if you ask me," said the face. "We can't feed the whole world, let alone some Johnny-come-lately long-lost son who shows up at the last minute before times really get tight on Number Day."

"He was such a dreamer. You couldn't tell him anything. He left a good job for a bunch of toys," said Uncle Bill's face.

"But it's not true!" John shouted out. He ran over to the talking faces. "You know that's not really true!" John protested.

"I'm leaving, Joe," a woman's voice said angrily. "I can't take it anymore. We gave up everything we dreamed of, everything we hoped for. They've beat us. I just can't take it."

John blinked in surprise when he realized it was the face of his mother talking. She looked very upset.

"No," John said. "She loves you. Deep down she has to love you. You're married."

"Nothing lasts forever," another voice said. John was surprised to see it was the head of his father, speaking to the head of his mother. "You didn't help me. But I wasn't worth helping, was I?"

"Stop fighting, please." John pleaded to the talking faces. "Tell her you didn't mean it, Daddy. Tell Mom you love her."

John ran to his father and shook him. But his father looked away. The crowd of talking faces only grew louder. But then one face spoke out above all the rest.

"Some people have good parents. Some people don't," the face of John Kramar said. "I was just one of those kids who had lousy parents. I don't know why I even bothered to look for him. It was all a waste of time. I was a lot better off without them."

John looked at his own face with surprise. His father's muddy head seemed to droop even lower in the dim light.

"I didn't mean it!" John cried out. "I said those things when I was hurt and mad."

"It's what I deserve," his father droned. "If I wasn't such a chicken, I would have ended it a long time ago. I should have died in that storm. But I made a deal. I sold out. I was afraid and I sold out."

"But you can come home," John pleaded. "You can start over again. I'll help you. We'll all help you."

"I can't leave," his father said, bowing his head. He sobbed softly. "I don't deserve to leave. I have to serve my time out like they said. Besides, I'm just no good."

John opened his mouth to plead with his father, but no words came out. Soon the walls of the pit were covered with talking faces, whispering words, hissing words. The room was filled with the great shameful weight of all the accusations. His father tried to cover his eyes and his ears at the same time.

"I'm just no good," his father moaned, shaking his head. "I wish I was dead. I've messed up my life forever."

"Then I'm staying with you, because I'm no good either," John said suddenly. "I'm not any good, really. I judged you, just like they've judged you. And you've judged yourself."

His father looked up in surprise. John stood defiantly before him.

"But you don't have to stay here," his father said. "You can leave. You haven't done anything wrong."

"Everybody's done something wrong," John replied. "So if you stay, I'll stay here with you. At least we'll keep each other company."

"Against the rules, against the rules," a voice suddenly shrieked on the wall. It was the head of his father with a pig's snout. The eyes glowed red as they stared at John. "You can't break the rules. This is solitary confinement. You cannot stay! Get out! Get out! Only one person is allowed per pit. You can't share them. I'm so sooooorrrrrrryyyyyyyyyyy."

John reached down and felt around his father's waist. He touched the chain. The dark links were wrapped around and around. John began searching for the end of the chain to see if there was a lock. But he could find none.

"There's no lock on this chain," John said. "It's wrapped around you, but there's no lock. Don't you see? You don't have to stay here."

"But this is where bad people stay," his father moaned. "I have to stay because I've been bad. I've been a bad person, a terrible father, and a worse husband and son. I'm not going anywhere. I'll be here forever this time."

John dipped the bucket into the mud. He picked it up and poured it over himself.

"No, John!" he father shouted, trying to take the bucket away.

"See, now I'm covered just like you," John said.

"What a little pig!" the voices screamed. "Two pigs in the pit."

With the mud and slop dripping down his face, John turned to his father and smiled.

"I'm still clean," John said happily. "Don't you see? I can be covered with mud on the outside, but on the inside I'm still clean because the Kingson made me clean where it counts, don't you see? It wasn't what we did or didn't do that made us clean, but what the Kingson did. He bought us back. He gave you his heart, don't you remember? I know you had a Spirit Flyer yourself a long time ago. You must remember."

"But I gave up my right to ride it," his father protested. "I turned my back on the kings."

"But they never turned their backs on you," John replied. Suddenly he knew what the keys were for. He slid the ring off his arm and held up one of the keys. He hadn't seen it before, but the name was there on the side of the first key: *Joe Kramar.*

"This is your key," John said. He pulled and the key came off the ring. In his hand, it began to glow and turn brighter gold in color. John's father stared at the gold key. He read his name written there.

The accusing loud voices began screeching even louder, repeating the same things. But John spoke out above the flaming words.

"Joe Kramar is the name on this key," John said loudly. And as soon as he had finished speaking, the key began to glow brighter and brighter, like the filament of a light bulb. The brighter it got, the better John felt just holding it. The whole muddy pit was filled with light. Soon the key was shining so brightly that they couldn't look at it.

Then the light dimmed. They blinked their eyes open with surprise. Instead of a key, John was now holding a shining golden helmet. *Joe Kramar* was written across the top. Three golden crowns were stamped into the metal, the sign of the Three Kings. John couldn't stop smiling.

"See?" he said. "This is a sign of your deliverance, that you indeed belong to the kings."

John jumped up on the soggy bed, then reached over and held the helmet over his father's muddy head. As John started to lower the golden helmet, flowing water suddenly gushed out over his father.

In an instant, all the mud and slop began to wash off. The gracious water flooded out, sparkling like drops of living jewels, covering his whole body. In less than a minute, he was soaking wet and very, very clean.

"I told you he makes us clean, again and again," John said. Then he lowered the wonderful golden helmet onto his father's head.

As soon as the helmet rested on his head, all the loud accusing voices stopped speaking. The dark chain wrapped around his waist uncoiled like a dead snake and fell to the floor with a rattle. Joe looked down at the heap of dead links of the chain as if he couldn't believe it. The whole room was still. Joe Kramar was speechless. With his head covered with the shining golden helmet, his face began to show a new sense of peace. He looked down at his clean clothes. He touched his arm, almost as if to see if it was really clean.

"Maybe there is hope," Joe Kramar whispered at last. "But we're still in this pit."

John looked around. There were no doors. The deep darkness hovered above them like a heavy lid.

"There has to be a way out," John said. "The kings would never let us stay in a place like this. We don't have to stay here. We don't belong here."

John took another golden key. He grabbed his father's hand.

"We're leaving," John said firmly.

"But how?" his father asked. "There're no doors."

"The kings open doors where there don't seem to be any doors," John said simply. "I've seen it happen before. They make ways to escape when it seems impossible. They gave me more keys. I know there has to be a way."

John looked at the golden keys. One of the smaller ones seemed to glow. He held it in his hand.

"Let's go," John said. He walked straight for the wall of the pit. He held up the golden key before them. He kept walking without hesitation. When the key touched the wall, there was a flash of light. The wall suddenly seemed like nothing more than a curtain of smoke. John walked through, leading his father by the hand. John squinted as the smoke disappeared, then gasped at what he saw.

THE FATHER'S HOUSE
· · · · · · · ·
16

John blinked and rubbed his eyes. He'd assumed that they would be somewhere in Goliath Gardens. But instead they were in a magnificent room of a kind that he'd never seen before or even imagined. Both he and his father stared in surprise.

"This is some kind of palace," his father whispered at last.

"Yeah," John said softly. "What a place!"

The size of the palace and the colors were what took John by surprise. They were in a very large room, as big as a gymnasium. A huge crystal chandelier burned with light that was sharp and pure and clean. Everything was bright and alive. The floor was a golden color, and the walls

seemed to be made of a kind of glass that reminded John of the diamond ring his aunt wore. But the best thing of all was the atmosphere of the house. Everything was totally peaceful and calm. A beautiful fragrance filled the air.

"This is the most beautiful place I've ever seen," Joe Kramar whispered in awe. "But you know, I feel so at home. I feel like I belong here. But I don't ever remember being here before."

"I feel the same way," John said. He squeezed his father's hand. "I feel like it's home too. It seems like I've been here before, but I would have remembered being in this place."

A sound seemed to be coming from a door to their left. "Let's see who lives here," John said excitedly. Both father and son walked at first and then began to run across the long room toward the door. The more they ran, the better they felt. With each step, the joy of running and being in that place increased. They were whooping and laughing by the time they reached the door.

When they looked through, their mouths fell open. Neither man nor boy said anything for a long moment. At the threshold of the door, they peered into the largest and most magnificent room they had ever seen. It seemed to go on for miles. And right in the center of the room was a sparkling table. The table seemed to fill the room even into the far distance. Splendid chairs surrounded the table, and at each place, magnificent dishes were set out and waiting. John had never seen such dishes before.

"Welcome to my Father's house," a voice said behind them. John and his father turned.

Both dropped to their knees at the sight of the Kingson. Then John realized what he had known in his heart all along. This was the palace of the Kingson himself. Joe Kramar began to shake and cry. John reached over and patted him on the back. Compassion and kindness flowed out of the Kingson's eyes as he looked down at John's father.

"I'm so unworthy, so unworthy," his father sobbed at the feet of the

Kingson. But the Kingson reached down and very tenderly touched the weeping man on the back.

"Stand up, Joe Kramar," the Kingson said firmly. Then he looked at John. Without asking, John knew he was supposed to stand, also.

John and his father stood up, but his father continued to look away from the gaze of the Kingson. But John was watching everything.

"We're wearing different clothes," John said. He didn't know how or when it had happened, but both he and his father were wearing new clothes that seemed to be made of the finest blue and purple cloth. The golden helmet was no longer on his father's head. Instead, a golden key hung on a thin golden chain around his neck.

John's father looked down at himself. He had new shoes on his feet and clothes to match.

"But I don't deserve this," Joe Kramar said. "I don't understand. I don't understand why we are here."

"You're here because you were invited from the beginning," the Kingson said. "You heard the invitation and you accepted."

"But I don't feel like I belong," Joe Kramar said, a troubled look on his face. "Part of me feels at home, and the other part feels like a trespasser or a thief."

"What I call worthy is worthy," the Kingson said simply, but with great authority. "What I've cleaned is cleaned, and what I love is lovable. No one can give himself worth in his own eyes. Only the greater can give worth to something lesser. My Father and I cherish both of you. You are very precious and valuable to me, Joe Kramar. Joe Kramar, you are a treasure in my heart and in my Father's heart."

"I think I understand," John said excitedly. "It's sort of like gold. Gold is only a metal, but because it's rare and people want it, it has value. Some people will do anything to get gold. They'll even die trying. But if people didn't want gold, it wouldn't be worth anything."

"You are much more precious to me and my Father than gold," said the Prince of Kings. "Gold is a lifeless thing. When you were dead and lifeless, I gave you my very life so we could share our lives forever."

Joe Kramar looked up into the face of the Kingson with new eyes. He looked at his clean hands and the fine clothes. He began to see himself as the Prince of Kings saw him. And for the first time in many years, he liked what he saw.

"You did all this for me?" he asked in a whisper. "But why?"

"Why do any parents want their children? You make my joy complete by turning away from death and accepting my gift of life," the Kingson said with a smile. "My joy is to share every good gift I have with you as the Father of Kings has shared with me. The Father is most pleased to share everything that he has with his sons and daughters. He wants his house to be filled with many, many children."

Joe Kramar took a deep breath. His heart was pounding with life. He squeezed his hands into fists and then relaxed.

"This is great!" he said excitedly. "It's as if I've been blinded all this time and forgot I was a son. I've been living like an orphan, like someone who didn't even know his own father."

"This is great news, isn't it?" John agreed. Father and son smiled at each other.

"I remember feeling like this once before," Joe Kramar said. "This is the way it was at the beginning, before . . . before I stopped trusting . . . that you would take care of everything."

Joe looked sadly into the eyes of the Kingson. The Kingson looked back, his eyes both understanding and forgiving.

"No matter what you do, you will always be your Father's son," the Prince of Kings replied. "You made many mistakes, Joe. And you may make some more. The Father and I feel great sorrow when any of our children suffer. But you've always had a place in the Father's house. This is your true home and that's never changed. All of those children who are born into his kingdom will live with him forever, and nothing can take them away from his house. Neither death nor life, neither height nor depth can separate you from the love of your Father the King."

143

"I read something about that in the Book of the Kings," John said excitedly, squeezing his father's hand. "Now I'm beginning to understand what I read."

"You've been away from your Father's house, wandering down many roads," the Kingson said. "But now you're welcomed home. You always have a place here. At my table, a place is set for you. Soon, we'll all have a feast together."

The Kingson pointed at the long table. John licked his lips. He wondered what kind of food would be on the menu in such a wonderful place. "Wow," John said softly. "I can hardly wait for that."

"I don't know why I stayed away so long," Joe Kramar said. "I can't believe I let myself get so deceived. But what about Mary? I know she's in trouble, too. Can't you help her?"

"Yes. Please help my mother get well," John added.

"She's another one left in prison, locked in her shame," the Kingson said, looking at John and his father. "But you have the key to free her."

"We do?" John asked.

"Let's go," Joe said. "I can't wait to tell her what's happened!"

"Follow me," the Kingson said. He walked across the room. Both John and his father were right behind the Prince of Kings.

As he got closer to the wall, the Kingson seemed to be looking at something. He stopped.

"There she is," he said. "She's waiting."

"Where?" John and his father asked together.

"Right there," the Kingson pointed. And when his arm was outstretched, they saw deeper in the direction where he was pointing. Instantly they were in a dark clammy room with gray stone walls that resembled an old dungeon. Water dripped down the dungeon walls onto the cold stone floor. She was directly in front of them, against the far wall. A large black snake was wrapped around her waist. The snake was wrapped so tightly it almost seemed to be a part of her.

"Feed me. Feed me," the snake demanded. Then the coils of the great snake began to squeeze her waist and stomach so hard that she doubled over in pain and cried out.

"Feed me, you fool, or I'll kill you now," the serpent demanded.

With shaking pale hands, the woman held out two white pills. She lowered them to the snake's mouth. The mouth opened greedily and then bit down on her hand and wrist.

"Aaahhh," she moaned in pain. The snake then loosened its grip, but just a little. That's when the Kingson strode forward. For the first time, the snake seemed to notice that visitors had entered its dungeon.

The ugly dark serpent reared back and spread its hood. The mouth opened, showing glistening red fangs, dripping with poison. The Kingson stared into the red eyes of the serpent with disgust. "You are trespassing in my territory," the serpent said to the Kingson.

"Wherever I go, my Kingdom follows," the Prince of Kings replied. "And this dungeon is now my territory. And this woman is my child, and a subject of my Kingdom."

"You helped put her here," the serpent hissed out, looking directly at John's father. "You have no right to be here. You caused most of the problems yourself. How dare you try to defy me?"

Joe Kramar looked down at his feet. For a moment he was quiet, as if unsure of himself. Then he looked up and faced the mocking serpent.

"I did make some mistakes, and so did my wife," Joe Kramar said evenly. "But I'm still a child of the kings, and the Kingdom is in this place now. My wife is a child of the kings, too. In the name of the kings and by their authority, I'm telling you to get out and leave her alone, now!"

Joe Kramar blinked in surprise at the sound of his own voice. The snake hissed once and began to smoke. Mary Kramar coughed loudly.

"Stop tormenting her!" Joe Kramar commanded in a louder voice. The smoke lifted. A dark pool of tar was on the floor near his wife's feet. John and his father ran to her. She fell limply into her husband's arms and seemed to be asleep. The Kingson smiled at the family.

Then the Prince of Kings looked down at the black tarry pool on the stone floor. Instantly the pool began to boil and burst into flames. Screeching voices bubbled up out of the fire, but in a few seconds, the voices and tarry pool had all been burned away. Not a trace or a stain was left.

Joe Kramar carried his wife away from the prison wall. John Kramar lifted his mother's feet. Before they realized it, they were back inside the kings' palace. John and his father were surprised to see how quickly their surroundings had changed. A bed was waiting. Joe Kramar laid his wife on the clean sheets. John and his father sat down beside the bed in two waiting chairs. The Kingson stood beside them.

"How did we get from your palace to that dungeon and then back again so quickly?" Joe Kramar asked. "Your palace walls seemed to be right next to that pit we were in, and also the dungeon walls."

"The Kingdom is always close to those who need it," the Kingson said. "Those who believe and have keys can find the way back to my Kingdom quickly, because it is near, just on the other side of any wall of fear or sorrow or death. The Kingdom is close, but so few remember how to press through into it. They give up and remain stuck behind the prison walls of their own choosing. But your wife is safe now."

Joe Kramar touched his wife's hand. Already, the color and life were coming back into her face. Mary Kramar moaned. Her hands reached down and touched her stomach. The she opened her eyes. She saw Joe and John with the Kingson standing behind them.

"You're here," she said weakly. She touched her stomach again. "The pain is gone."

"You're safe, Mary," Joe Kramar said tenderly. "The Kingson rescued you. And me too. We're in his house right now."

Mary Kramar looked around at the magnificent palace walls. She took a deep breath of the fragrant air. Then she sighed.

"I'm so tired," she said.

"You need to rest," Joe said, touching her forehead.

"I want to go home now," Mary said dreamily. "What time is it?"

"It's five o'clock," John Kramar said. The instant he spoke, everything began to change. Suddenly he and his father were outside the walls of Goliath Gardens. The tall hills of the Goliath roller coaster rose up against the sky. John looked around in surprise. He could still smell the refreshing fragrant air of the palace of the kings. Both he and his father were sitting on red Spirit Flyer bicycles. The Kingson stood behind his father.

"What happened?" John asked. "Where did my mother go?"

"Your mother is safe now," the Kingson said. "She's resting."

"But where did the palace go?" John asked. "We were right there."

"You never leave the presence of the Father and his house," the Kingson said simply.

"But I don't see it anymore," John replied. He squinted, looking around.

"You have to look deeper," the Kingson said. "You'll see it in a little while, but now it's time to go back to Centerville. Your family is waiting for you."

Joe Kramar looked down at his Spirit Flyer bicycle. His eyes were wet with tears as he softly touched the old horn and the gear lever. "I thought I'd never see this old bicycle again," Joe Kramar said.

"Some children never receive their gifts, and others misuse them or even try to sell them," the Kingson said. "But the Father's heart is one that gives and hopes. Don't be imprisoned in the past. You're out of that pit. Take with thanksgiving what's been given to you. Enjoy and use your gifts with the pleasure and spirit in which they were given."

Joe Kramar looked into the Kingson's loving eyes. In the silence, he could smell the fragrant air of the kings' palace again.

"Thank you for giving this wonderful bicycle to me," Joe Kramar said to the Prince of Kings.

"The pleasure is mine," the Kingson replied.

Both father and son began to pedal the old red bicycles. Side by side they headed north. John was the first one to aim his bike up toward the clouds. Joe Kramar hesitated. Then he too pointed his handlebars toward the sky. The big balloon tires left the earth. For a moment he seemed afraid of falling off. But in an instant, the joy of riding all came back to him. No one, he realized, ever could forget how to ride a Spirit Flyer. He shot higher into the air and was soon riding side by side with his son.

"Beat you home!" John shouted to his father.

"Not if I get there first," his father replied. With whoops and joyful shouts, both boys, one slightly older than the other, stood up on the pedals and raced upward to the clouds. They were still laughing when they reached the farmhouse on Glory Road.

A
LONG
TALK
· · · · · · · · ·
17

Grandfather Kramar was outside in front of the workshop when the two bike riders got home. The old man's face beamed when he saw John and Joe on their Spirit Flyer bicycles.

"I knew something good was happening," Grandfather Kramar shouted. He ran once again to his son. "I knew the Kingson would bring you back to us."

The two men embraced. John jumped off his bicycle and joined in.

"Dad, I'm sorry for everything," Joe Kramar said. "I have so much to tell you. So much has happened. I want to tell you the whole story."

"Well, why don't you save it for now?" Grandfather Kramar said. "I'm sure Bill and Betty want to hear it too. Right now there's good news. Mary has had a dramatic turnaround for the good. The hospital called just after five o'clock and told us she was doing much better. They were all surprised. Bill and Betty went right over. I was just getting ready to go myself."

"Let's all go," John said.

They were all heading to the old pickup truck when the Kramars' car pulled into the driveway. Bill honked the horn. He was smiling when he got out. Betty ran over to Joe and John, carrying little Paul Nathaniel.

"She's going to be all right," Betty said with a huge grin. "She's real tired and sleepy, right now, but she's going to be okay, the doctors said. They think that she can even come home in a few days. Oh, Joe, it's wonderful. It's like a miracle."

"We saw her," John said to his aunt. "We saw my mom too."

"When?" Grandfather Kramar asked.

"It's kind of hard to explain," Joe Kramar said slowly.

"Well, let's go in the house and make some tea," Grandfather Kramar said. "I guess there's a lot that needs to be told."

The Kramars all went inside the house. Grandfather Kramar put the teakettle on. John made several pieces of toast with butter and cinnamon on top and put them on a big blue plate. Everyone sat around the kitchen table. Grandfather Kramar poured the tea. Aunt Betty bounced Paul Nathaniel on her knees.

"I know I have a lot of explaining to do," Joe Kramar said seriously.

"Before you say anything, I want you to know that I'm really glad you're back," Bill Kramar said to his younger brother. "I don't care what happened or what went wrong. I'm just glad you're here now. I made some judgments and said some things I regret. Please forgive me."

Bill Kramar reached over toward his brother. The two men hugged for a long time.

"I'd like your forgiveness too," Joe said softly. "I owe you all an explanation. I'm not sure where to begin. I guess I should start right about the time before the storm."

The back door slammed. Cousin Lester and Lester, Jr., walked into the kitchen.

"Oh, the prodigal has returned again," Cousin Lester said dryly. "Wonders never cease. I see you're having tea. I'll just pour myself a cup."

"I don't have to drink that awful tea, do I, Daddy?" Les, Jr., whined.

"No. You can go on up to your room," Cousin Lester said. He sat down as Les, Jr., ran out of the room. He stared down his long thin nose at Joe Kramar.

"Right before the storm, I met a man named Grinsby," Joe Kramar said. "I had opened the toy store and was making toys. But things hadn't turned out like I'd expected with the toy business. I loved making things and having the store, but it was harder to get a business going than I figured. Teaching school was a lot more stable."

"Government jobs can be a real blessing," Cousin Lester said. He sipped loudly from his cup of tea.

"Anyway, this man named Grinsby came into the store one day," Joe Kramar continued. "He was particularly interested in our Spirit Flyer bicycles. He wanted to buy them, but I wouldn't sell. We hadn't had them very long. I tried to explain them to the two of you," Joe said looking at Uncle Bill and Aunt Betty, "but you didn't seem to believe me when I told you they could fly and do amazing things."

"We just thought the whole thing was crazy," Uncle Bill said. "I even told Betty you'd gone off the deep end."

"Well, I got into everything deeper and deeper, including debt," Joe said. "When Grinsby came the second time, I listened to his offer a little more closely. I don't know what I was thinking. I felt like a failure. Bill always seemed so stable and sure of himself. He had told me that going into the toy business was a silly dream, especially since I had had a stable job teaching school."

Bill Kramar nodded his head sadly. "I guess I was too hasty too," he said to Joe. "Maybe I could have helped you more."

"My dream was to own the store," Joe said. "But the bills have to be paid, even in dreams. Right around then, Mary hurt her back helping me lift a big doll house. We didn't have medical insurance and the hospital bills were expensive. Her back kept hurting, so they gave her some pain medication. The dosage was high. When she came home from the hospital, I had my hands full. I was trying to run the house, trying to run the store and trying to build toys."

"I didn't know Mary got hurt," Betty said.

"We didn't tell anyone," Joe replied. "I was still angry because Bill didn't believe me about the Spirit Flyers. And I didn't want to admit I was going through a hard time with my business, especially after he had warned me not to leave my teaching job. Anyway, to make a long story short, things got worse and I got very discouraged.

"About that same time, one of Mary's old friends from high school had a baby girl. But there were problems from the beginning, and the baby died from a rare disease. These friends, the Landons, had Spirit Flyers too. We all used to go out riding together. But they were really upset after their baby's death, and so were we. Mary wanted us to have more stability in our life. She still had problems with her back. She was taking more and more medicine for the pain. We were both scared for different reasons. Then Grinsby came back again, offering me a lot of money for the bicycles. This time the offer looked like a way out of a lot of pain and misery."

The room was quiet. John had barely eaten any of his toast. Cousin Lester poured himself another cup of tea.

"Well, I told Mary about the offer," Joe said. "She was suspicious, but I told her we needed to do something. I didn't believe that the kings would help us like it says in the Book of the Kings, especially after the Landons' baby died. I felt more bitter and discouraged than ever. Finally Grinsby offered more money, and I convinced Mary that we should take him up on his offer. I thought we could get enough money to pay off our bills, get Mary's back looked at by a specialist and so on. I thought all our problems would be solved."

"I've heard that before," Cousin Lester said.

"It had been stormy and rainy all week," Joe Kramar said. "Tornadoes were spotted in several places. But one time, I saw a tornado that was more than a tornado. It was a giant, black cobralike snake."

"I remember you telling me," Bill Kramar said. "I didn't believe you about that either."

"Well, who would believe a crazy story like that?" Cousin Lester sniffed. "I've never heard of such a thing."

"I should have seen it as a warning, but I didn't," Joe continued. "That evening, just around dark, we went to meet Grinsby. I was ready to sell out. We left John with some friends because I didn't want him around Grinsby. We headed out of town when the winds really hit. Grinsby was waiting for us. We pulled over to the side of the road behind his black truck. Our bicycles were in the trunk."

"He had a black truck when he was here last year, remember?" John asked.

"Grinsby had a big envelope full of money," Joe said. "I rolled the bicycles into the back of his truck. Then he said we had to sign something, a piece of paper. Well, the wind was getting worse. Mary and I wanted to leave, but Grinsby insisted. So we got in his truck. As soon as he closed the door, this horrible-smelling gas covered us, and we passed out."

"Oh, really!" Cousin Lester said. "Do you expect us to believe that? What nonsense!"

"Go on," Grandfather Kramar said. He frowned at Cousin Lester.

"The next thing we knew, we woke up in this terrible place," Joe said. "Mary and I were only half awake, it seemed, but the whole thing was like a nightmare. We were as close to being scared to death as we'd ever been. Grinsby made us sign documents with drops of our own blood.

Then he told us we were his prisoners and that he owned our chains, and if we tried to escape, he would kill us and kill John also."

"Wow," John said.

"Mary and I were so scared, we didn't know what to believe," Joe said. "Right then I should have called out to the kings, but I was too ashamed. I had already sold their gifts for money and a drop of blood. Grinsby threatened us again. He showed us our car. Right before our eyes, a tornado came down and destroyed it. Then he said he would hurt John if we didn't obey him. He even said that he and his group had been responsible for the death of the Landons' baby. He told us so many details about it that we began to believe him."

Joe stopped to get a drink of tea. He took a deep breath.

"Grinsby told us that we would be assumed dead, killed in the storm," Joe continued. "His threats seemed so real. So we agreed to go with him. I was scared and ashamed for the mess I'd gotten us in. I began to believe that John was better off without us. I knew that Bill and Betty would take care of him. At first I thought we could escape after a while.

"But things got worse," Joe said. "One bad choice led to another and another. Link by link I wrapped myself and Mary up into a bigger chain. Grinsby took us to this horrible Goliath factory a thousand miles away from Centerville. Instead of making toys, I was working on this miserable assembly line making parts for some kind of weapons that Goliath builds. We had barely any money, and no self-respect. We lived in a tiny barracks apartment that Goliath owned.

"Mary's back pains got worse, so she took more and more medicine to ease the pain. Then the Goliath doctors started giving her a new medicine. It made her feel better, but she got so she couldn't stand to live without it. Neither one of us wanted to admit how dependent she was on this medicine. Our plans to escape just frittered away as time passed. There didn't seem to be any way out. We both felt like total failures. We were convinced John would be better off without us."

John Kramar nibbled his toast quietly. Bill reach out and patted Joe's arm.

"The weeks turned into months, then a year and then years," Joe said. "We worked wherever Goliath told us. One time we came by Centerville. Mary was in pain and took some of those Z-Pops. I went into town and asked a few questions. I found out John was doing OK, so I was satisfied. We just went on. I was too ashamed to make any real contact. I believed everyone was better off thinking we were dead. At least no one would know what a failure I turned out to be.

"Our last job was at Goliath Gardens," Joe continued. "It was the most pitiful one, but I felt like we deserved it. In the winter we would travel with the carnival. Mary played one of the grave ladies, and I played one of the crazy hogmen. I thought I'd be in that slop pile the rest of my life, I guess. After giving up all hope and any of the self-respect I had left, it seemed like the natural job for me.

"When the Halloween War came, I was just glad to have a job. I was thinking about coming back by Centerville this year once we got settled in again at Goliath Gardens. But I don't know that I would have done it. Then one day, Mary just up and left.

"I didn't blame her for leaving me. I was always surprised she didn't leave sooner. She'd lost most of her self-respect because she knew she had to have those Z-Pops. That's about the only thing that really mattered to her for the last two years. If she took them, she could do her job. But she'd get more and more depressed, sometimes for weeks at a time. She'd have nightmares. I'd hear her talking in her sleep. Finally, she just took off.

"She'd been gone for three weeks before John showed up on Saturday. I was never more ashamed in my life to have my own son see me standing in the middle of that slop pile. Still, I decided I wanted to come home too."

The kitchen was quiet. Even Cousin Lester didn't seem to have anything to say.

"When I got here, I was glad, but the shame and disgust I felt was even worse," Joe said. "I just didn't think I could tell anyone the whole truth. Then I heard Bill and Lester talking after supper. I just couldn't face it, so I ran away again. I knew I'd let everybody down. I was sorry I had given John or Dad reason to hope since I felt like I was a such hopeless person. I didn't want John to look at me as an example of a father."

Bill looked down at his folded hands. He frowned. John stood up. He walked around the table and sat in his father's lap and hugged him around the neck. Joe Kramar's eyes filled with tears.

Betty Kramar stood up. She wiped her eyes with her apron. She put on a fresh pot of hot water for tea. John continued to hang on his father's neck. Then he looked at his father with a smile.

"But tell them the good part," John said finally. "Tell them how we got out of that pit. Tell about the kings' palace, and about how we saw Mom."

As fresh cups of tea were poured, Joe began telling the rest of the story. When he slowed down, John would fill in other details. As everyone realized what the kings had done for Joe and Mary, they began to smile in amazement. When John told them about seeing his mother at exactly five o'clock, Aunt Betty whooped in surprise and delight.

"Then it is true," Aunt Betty exclaimed. "The Kingson really did deliver her from that awful stuff."

"The hospital said it would be doing tests all this week," Uncle Bill said. "But it looks good."

"I've heard all I can stand of this nonsense," Cousin Lester said. He glared at Joe Kramar with hard glinting eyes. "How can you believe this pack of lies from someone who deserted his child and stayed away for years? How can you welcome him back into this house? Besides, where will we put another two adults? My room is already crowded as it is. I can't believe you'd listen to this hard luck baloney story, right when our whole country is in crisis. This farm is in a crisis too. We'll all be hurting soon enough without two more adults to support. Why should we all suffer because this wayward son wants to mooch off us, after all the terrible, disgusting things he's done?"

"This whole place used to be Joe's farm, or did you forget that?" Grandfather Kramar said. John was surprised. He had hardly ever seen his grandfather get angry before. But there was a storm brewing in the old man's gaze.

"But he gave it up," Cousin Lester sniffed. "He gave up everything, and now he wants it back, handed to him on a silver platter as if nothing had ever happened."

"I never said that," Joe Kramar responded, looking confused.

"You just come home and say you're sorry and think that makes everything fine and dandy, don't you?" Cousin Lester demanded.

"I wasn't trying to say that," Joe replied. "I was just trying to explain what happened. I didn't say it made everything all right. I know there are a lot of things we'll have to sort through."

"And we'll do it together," Grandfather Kramar said. "We'll all learn how to do it together, and with the kings' help and love, we'll turn this situation around."

"Well, let me tell you my opinion about that," Cousin Lester said. His face was very red. "I don't intend to—"

"You don't need to say anything else," a deep voice cut in. Every head turned. Standing in the doorway of the kitchen was the Kingson himself. He had suddenly appeared without anyone noticing, but now all eyes were fastened on him. "I want to talk with you."

The Kingson was looking directly at Cousin Lester. Even Lester had a hard time looking back into the eyes of the Kingson.

"Talk to me?" Cousin Lester asked feebly.

"Yes, outside, behind the barn, away from this family," the Kingson said firmly.

Suddenly John was tremendously happy he wasn't in Cousin Lester's shoes. Cousin Lester wiped his glasses nervously with a napkin.

"Go get your son and bring him with you," the Kingson said. "I will be waiting for both of you behind the barn."

No one said anything because there was nothing to say. There was no question that the Kingson would have to be obeyed. Cousin Lester gulped uneasily.

"Ahhhh . . . yes, sir, . . . I'll . . . ahhhh . . . go get him right away," Cousin Lester stammered. He looked terrified as he darted out of the room.

The Kingson turned and faced the rest of the family. Kindness and compassion filled his face once again.

"What are you going to do with Cousin Lester?" John asked eagerly. "I bet he's in big trouble."

The minute he asked, he regretted it. The Kingson stared quietly at John. The whole room was so still, it seemed as if no one was breathing.

"What I have to say to Lester is between him and me," the Kingson said. John understood clearly. What was going to happen was none of his business.

The Kingson turned and disappeared before their eyes. John ran to the window. Outside, Cousin Lester was walking quickly across the lawn toward the barn, dragging Les, Jr., by the hand. Though John couldn't hear him, he could tell that Les, Jr., was complaining all the way. They both disappeared behind the barn.

The whole family was watching. A flash of light shot up from behind the barn. Even with the windows closed, John heard two distinct voices crying out for a second.

"This is the kings' business," Grandfather Kramar said seriously. "We better step away from the window, or we'll be back behind the barn with Lester."

"Will they be all right?" John asked. He couldn't help but look one more time.

"The Kingson knows how to take care of things, wouldn't you agree?" his grandfather asked, a twinkle in his eye.

"Yeah," John said softly. He quickly stepped away from the window.

"I'll get some more tea and make more toast."

Thirty minutes later, the family was all enjoying another fresh cup of tea, when Lester and Les, Jr., walked in. The change on their faces was remarkable. Cousin Lester immediately walked up to Joe Kramar and began to mumble.

"What?" Joe Kramar asked.

"I said that I made a big mistake in judging you, and I'd appreciate your forgiveness," Cousin Lester said sheepishly. He looked at Les, Jr. "In fact, me and Les, here, have decided to make a little room out in the workshop. You can use my room, I mean John's room. He's been kind of stuck up in the attic through no fault of his own. I, ahh, . . . want to apologize to you all if I have said or done things that haven't been kind or loving. What I mean to say, is that I'm sorry for acting . . . for acting . . ."

"For acting like a jerk," Les, Jr., said. "That's the way the Kingson said it, didn't he?"

Cousin Lester's face turned red. "More or less," he replied. "Anyway, I guess we better get packing some things here and move on out to the workshop."

Joe Kramar nodded and said, "Sure, I forgive you, Les." Cousin Lester and Les, Jr., quickly shuffled out of the room. John looked at the others. He wondered why he was the only one smiling.

"Wait up, Cousin Lester," John called out with a grin. "I'll help you!"

No one said anything else. No one was sure what happened that day with the Kingson and Cousin Lester and Les, Jr., behind the barn. But nobody asked either. After all, it was the kings' business.

EASTER SUNDAY

18

The rest of that week passed quickly for the Kramar family. Each day was a fresh adventure. Two more families arrived to camp on the edge of the south pasture as Number Day was about to start.

In several places around the country, there were protests and disturbances. The Kramar family watched the news like everyone else. In each place, the ORDER Security Squads squashed the protesters. Cash and coins had become almost totally worthless, except to collectors. All the stores demanded payment by the Point System.

Centerville was like most towns. There was no big disturbance. Most people had already shifted over to the number cards and the Point System.

Joe and Bill Kramar began to dig some new wells and new ponds that week, anticipating the need for more water for the Pasture People, as they now called them.

The crops showed their early green in the fields. The campers in the pasture provided plenty of willing hands to work. Some got jobs on nearby farms. They agreed to be paid in food and other supplies.

Early on Easter Sunday morning, Mary Kramar was released from the hospital. Joe and Bill Kramar drove her home. Though she still seemed tired, her eyes were clear and bright.

When she got to the Kramar place, she was surprised to see hundreds of old red bicycles parked everywhere. A huge celebration was taking place in the pasture behind the workshop. The people all sang louder as Mary and Joe arrived.

After a while, Grandfather stood up to talk. Everyone got quiet.

"This is the day we celebrate the new life the Kingson won for us all by conquering death once and for all!"

The crowd cheered and clapped and began singing again. Men and children danced in circles. Mary and Joe Kramar linked arms and began to dance too. Everyone was caught up in the celebration honoring the Kingson and his triumph over death.

Then the people got quiet again. Grandfather Kramar smiled as he looked out at all the faces. He walked over and patted Joe and Mary Kramar on the back.

"I want to thank the kings for bringing these two out of a terrible pit and back home where they belong," Grandfather Kramar said. His voice cracked. "We all thought they were dead. And in a way, they lived like those who are dead and without hope. But Joe and Mary are a living testimony that no matter how many mistakes you make and no matter how unworthy you feel, the Kingson is faithful even when we are not. He will go out and find every one of his children who are lost. If you

cry out for help, he will hear you and lead you home. And I rejoice in the presence of everyone here that these two have been led back home. No matter what happens in the future, we can be at peace, knowing the kings will always lead us in the paths of life that will take us home."

The crowd went wild, singing and rejoicing again. The dancing and songs seemed to last forever. And as they praised the King of Kings, the Kingson himself stood in the middle of their dancing. When they saw him, the shouts of joy were even louder.

John had never known that Easter could be this way. He linked arms with old friends from town and new friends from the Pasture People.

Food was served. This feast was twice as big as when John's father had come home. Everyone had plenty to eat.

As people gathered to sing again, the Kingson stood in their midst. Suddenly, for a brief moment, they all found themselves dancing and singing inside a tremendously large and magnificent room. The whole crowd was caught up into the light and glory of the place. No one spoke. They stared in awe at the beauty, smelling the fragrant fresh air, feeling the royal presence of the Father of Kings himself.

"This is the kings' palace that I told you about," John shouted excitedly to his friend Daniel. Everyone began to talk at once as they explored the royal mansion. Each person oohed and aahed as they all peeked into the great feast room where the dishes were waiting on the giant table.

"This is the most fantastic place I've ever seen," Daniel Bayley said. Amy Burke nodded. Her eyes were wide with surprise as she stared at each new sight. The Prince of Kings smiled and greeted each person. Every one, young and old, rich or poor, felt welcomed and wanted and loved. Each person felt like a child again, going inside the Father's house. In the next room they knew they would someday see him, and he would be glad to see them. The whole house was filled with his loving presence.

Then, as suddenly as they had been in the palace, they were back in the south pasture all together again.

"Wow!" Daniel said with awe. "Did you see what I just saw?"

Amy just whistled.

"Do you believe it?" John asked excitedly. "That was the second time I saw the Father's house."

All over the field, people had stopped to talk with one another, sharing what they had seen and what the Kingson had said to them.

"I wish we never had to leave," John said sadly. "Everything just seems to come and go so quickly, and I don't understand." He turned to say something else to Daniel but instead came face to face with the Kingson once again. The Kingson was smiling. Without a word, he reached over and touched John on his forehead.

In an instant, the boy's eyes were opened, and he saw deeper. Once again he saw the Father's magnificent house. He realized that he and all the other people in the pasture were still in the palace. But all around, on the palace walls he saw the farm, the house, the pasture, the trees and even the people. Only this time, the pasture and the barn and the house looked like part of a dim, watery movie, projected onto the walls. The flickering lights of this world suddenly seemed thin and temporary in contrast to the solid walls of the Father's house. Deep in his heart, John began to realize that he couldn't really leave the Father's house because that was where he lived; it was his true address and destiny. No matter what shadowy movie was playing itself out in the world, the Kingdom would remain forever and ever. His Father's house would be his true home.

"This is so great!" John said to the Kingson. "But this is Number Day. What will happen tomorrow to all of us?"

"Once you've seen deeper into the Father's house, the temporary places and changes in this life won't make you feel so lost," the Kingson said simply. "You always know the true direction home."

John was suddenly overwhelmed with a great sense of contentment and peace. He knew that being with the Kingson was the main thing.

Everything else would work out somehow. Finally, he knew what home was all about. John didn't say anything. He looked into the loving eyes of his king. He bowed before him. When he looked up, he was back in the pasture again. But deep in his heart, he knew he was really somewhere else too. He could still smell the fragrant air of the palace.

Everyone was still talking about what they had seen. But they wanted to do more than talk. Soon the air was filled with Spirit Flyer bicycles and other gifts. Young or old, no one was ashamed to be seen having fun. They were all like children playing in their Father's Kingdom.

John shot up into the air between his dad and Daniel Bayley. They circled out far past the boundaries of the farm. Some were already playing flight tag, others were just whizzing along as fast as they could go.

As they soared high above the clouds, the light was brilliant all around them. John grinned in the bright light. He wasn't sure whether it was the brightness of the sun or maybe just the twinkle of their Father's watching eye.